The Riddle of Time . . .

Here are stories of strange worlds, and stranger beings; of robots on this Earth, and off it; of man's newest element—space.

But space is only the stepping-stone to another element—time.

And Time is full of strange tricks.

So here also are richly imaginative tales of man's destiny in space—*and* in time; of one man who disconcertingly finds he is a ghost in the future before he has died in the present; of another who is trapped by time, in a most literal sense; of a third who is gloriously freed by time—and of men whose courage and drive to discover new dimensions forces them into a passage *through* time.

About Edmund Cooper and his first novel—

DEADLY IMAGE by Edmund Cooper. Ballantine Books, N. Y., 35¢

JACK Williamson once conjured up a paradise in which Man, served by robots, was freed at last of drudgery and economic insecurity. He showed, to the best of his ability, that such a heaven is but a step from hell. Cooper has raised the entire theme one level, populating his world with androids and humans. This change alone has altered the impact completely.

For some psychological reason, it is easy to imagine a robot world dedicated to service, however restrictive, to mankind. But androids, particularly articulate and adaptable ones, somehow strike the reader as a race apart, one that can conceivably compete with Man on a survival basis.

Cooper has seen the future in just that light. His oddly and aptly named atomic war, the "Nine Days Tranquilizer," has depopulated England to the extent that science perforce has had to develop artificial workers. From unskilled laborer to competent craftsman is merely a problem in time and evolution. Eventually, the androids become the backbone of society, administering as well as serving. Work and constructive activity are forbidden to humans.

John Markham, government refrigeration supervisor, is the unwilling and unhappy Survivor of the atomic age, deep-frozen at the cataclysmic moment. Revived and thrust unprepared into a leisurely paradise, all responsibility gone and all wants served by his own personal android, he still asks himself, with androids capable of all the physical and mental accomplishments of mankind, who needs Man?

Judged by this excellent first novel, Cooper is another fine new English talent to join the lengthening list of Ballantine discoveries. *Review from* GALAXY MAGAZINE

EDMUND COOPER

TOMORROW'S GIFT

BALLANTINE BOOKS, *New York*

Acknowledgments are due to the following magazines, in the pages of which these stories made their first appearance: AUTHENTIC SCIENCE FICTION (U.K.), FANTASTIC UNIVERSE (U.S.A.), JOHN BULL (U.K.), LONDON MYSTERY MAGAZINE (U.K.), OUTSPAN (South Africa), POCKET BOOK (Australia), SATURDAY EVENING POST (U.S.A.)

Library of Congress Catalog Card No. 58-13388

PRINTED IN CANADA

BALLANTINE BOOKS, INC.
101 Fifth Avenue, New York 3, N. Y.

CONTENTS

TOMORROW'S GIFT

Tomorrow's gift of joy or pain
renews the problem of desire.
Behind each vacant pair of eyes
lurks the sad prisoner of fire.

Anonymous Elizabethan Poet
Circa 1950.

From the twenty-seventh storey of the central administrative building the city looked like an enormous target, or a complex geometrical amoeba whose nucleus combined the functions of stomach, heart and brain.

Within this duodenal cerebrum were the co-ordinators, the architects of Nova Mancunia, the self-appointed masters of its fate. Their circular colony was exactly one mile in diameter for though there were no more than fifty co-ordinators to the total population of fifty thousand, they were careful to emphasize the privileges of rank.

Each co-ordinator lived according to his taste. Pre-Elizabethan farmhouses mingled with late Windsor mansions. A Norman church—rebuilt stone by stone, with the obvious addition of central heating and a swimming pool styled as a South Sea lagoon—lay facing an opaque glass windmill whose sails actually revolved. The most striking residence, perhaps, was that of the director. He chose to live in a replica of a nineteenth-century mill chimney, which perpetually belched forth a harmless synthetic smoke.

The central administrative building, the only functional element in the whole area, was no more than a hundred feet square and five hundred feet high. It was built entirely of stainless metal and plastic.

Surrounding the entire digestive braincenter of the city was a green belt, also a mile wide. It was a natural park where herds of deer appreciated, by simple analogy, the concept of a finite universe.

Beyond this again lay the mile-wide band which was the domain of five hundred technicians. Their accommodation was less ambitious than that of the co-ordinators and occupied less space. They lived in four different types of houses, according to status. There was the semi-detached cottage, the cottage, the cottage-residence and the residence.

Alpha technicians alone enjoyed the luxury of a residence and its indoor swimming pool. Altogether, there were fifty residences.

Exactly ninety-five per cent of the technicians' belt was occupied by electronic factories, power units and a hydroponics plant that, by itself, accounted for a thousand acres. The hydroponics installation, subdivided for convenience into five separate groups, produced Nova Mancunia's entire food supply—from yeast to yams, from apples to apricots, from milk substitute to synthetic mutton.

With the technicians' belt, the vital region of the city ended. Outside it there was another green belt and then the prefrontals' reservation—the territory reserved for numerous failed human beings. It was the home of men and women who were not illiterates but who were maladjusted. Some of them had been, potentially or actually, alpha technicians —even alpha co-ordinators. But they had become unhappy. Partial readjustment was simple; even the old pre-atomic surgeons were able to perform the operation of prefrontal leucotomy. A few brain fibers to be severed, the removal of a small amount of cerebral garbage—anxiety, doubt, resentment, despair—and then there was nothing to worry about. (Except that the patient was automatically sentenced to a life of happy retirement, his services being no longer required.)

Beyond the prefrontals' reservation was the epidermis of Nova Mancunia, the final layer of skin, the mass of the people. They lived in twenty-five glass and concrete hives, each containing one thousand flats. They lived and procreated and died. Their enormous blocks of flats were equally fertility symbols and tombstones.

Not being co-ordinators, or technicians, or prefrontals, they were classified as illiterates. Some of them were craftsmen or painters; some wrote imaginative histories or old-fashioned poems; some worked the land and produced unhygienic, unnecessary food; some designed clothes that would eventually wear out; and enough of them committed suicide to relieve the co-ordinators of the population problem.

Encircling this outer ring of hives was the wilderness, spotted here and there with other concentric cities; spotted also with round lakes whose waters would never drain away through their beds of glass and diamond. These were the monuments of the old hydrogen wars.

Six miles to the north was Lake Manchester. It had been one of the first cities to die.

8

Dr. Krypton gazed through his office window on the twenty-seventh storey of C.A.B. and watched the sails of the deputy director's glass windmill go round. It was his business to look for obscure meanings, and he wondered for the hundredth time if there was one here. Perhaps it was the deputy director's method of subtly announcing his deviationist tendencies. Certainly the sails described a revolution, impelled by a material force. Certainly the law governing the revolution had its sociological parallel. But would the deputy director be so subtle? Would he, also, with a tested happiness quotient of a hundred and fifty, and an intelligence quotient of a hundred and eighty, seek to change the status quo? Dr. Krypton dismissed these idle speculations with a shrug and turned to face the man in the room.

The visitor was a young man, under thirty—more than seventy years younger than the alpha psychiatrist who now confronted him.

He wore an air of aggressive resentment. But practically all Dr. Krypton's visitors did. It was either that or injured innocence.

What was the man's name? All Dr. Krypton could remember was that it was one he should have remembered. He glanced at the passport in his hands. *Byron, Mark Antony: Ph.D. Elec.: Technician Beta: H.Q. 105, I.Q. 115: D.O.B. 2473: Male.*

That was all the information. It was all that need be known. It was more than enough to distinguish Byron, Mark Antony, from Byron, Caesar Augustus—if there was one. For it was the story of a life.

"Why has your passport reached my office?" asked Dr. Krypton suddenly.

For a moment the young man's expression was blank, then he jerked out an answer: "I don't know, sir. I was about to ask you the same question."

It was the usual reaction. Dr. Krypton studied his patient objectively, wondering whether he would be likely to bore or entertain. A recommendation for immediate prefrontal would take care of the first possibility and an observation visa would provide for the latter.

"You know who I am, of course?" asked the psychiatrist briskly.

"Yes, sir. Co-ordinator alpha, consultant psychiatrist and neurosurgeon."

"You are aware of my H.Q./I.Q.?"

"One three five, and one seventy."

9

"Good, we shall perhaps save time. I have the advantage, I see, of fifty-five intelligence points. I have also the ultimate privilege of deciding your fate."

"I understand."

"I hope so. You, on the other hand, theoretically retain the choice of working with or against me. If you feel able to lie successfully, do so by all means. It will be a game of chess. You will play without a queen."

Dr. Byron appeared to pull himself together. He gazed at the psychiatrist coolly. "I presume my passport was sent to you because my efficiency is questioned?"

Dr. Krypton shook his head. "Reasons are never given. While I hold your passport you are my patient. You will provide the reasons."

"I could suggest a conspiracy."

"That would be tedious. Everyone does—even, on occasion, co-ordinators alpha. Fear temporarily decreases intelligence by perhaps twenty per cent."

"Suppose I have no fear?"

Dr. Krypton sighed. "When a man no longer has fear, he is acutely unhappy. I invariably recommend prefrontal."

Dr. Byron seemed suddenly to relax. He smiled. "As I am no longer afraid I accept both your diagnosis and treatment, sir. When may I expect the operation?"

The psychiatrist became interested. Here, at least, was an unusual approach. Many of those whose passports reached Dr. Krypton anticipated his recommendation and prepared for it in various ways—some by opening an artery and some by getting drunk. But here was one who seemed willing to short-circuit the entire analysis.

"You are in a hurry," observed Dr. Krypton. "Why do you want your present personality to die?"

The younger man appeared to restrain himself from laughing. "Isn't it already dead?"

"Demonstrably not."

"Then there is no time to lose. In the interests of communal stability you should amputate it as soon as possible."

"Why?"

"Because," said Dr. Byron calmly, "it generates delusions."

"Perhaps there is no future for anyone without them," suggested Krypton in a dry voice.

Dr. Byron raised his eyebrows. "Do you say that officially?"

It was the psychiatrist's turn to laugh. "Heresy has been

10

permitted for the *elite* ever since the Christian Church began the fashion. Officially, I may find it necessary."

Byron was silent for a moment. Then he spoke at great speed. "In the country of the blind, the one-eyed man is merely a psychotic. I am a psychotic, Dr. Krypton, because I do not share the reality of blindness. I am obsessed by the delusion of sight. I can see nothing but a slow disintegration in this stupid system of caste. On a planet that once supported three thousand million human beings there are now only ten million. They live in a couple of hundred hygienic Nova Mancunias. They do not procreate; they merely reproduce. I have discovered that there is a subtle difference. Has it occurred to you that in the last hundred years history has stopped? Nothing happens any more—nothing is lost and nothing is gained. All the Nova Mancunias everywhere are as dead and sterile as the lakes of the Hydrogen Wars. They are toy civilizations slowly running down. And there is no one to wind them up."

"Except you," said Krypton with sarcasm. "Why didn't you find a technician beta female, marry her, and sublimate these quixotic notions in an orderly domestic rhythm?"

"The classification of technician beta female supersedes that of woman," returned Byron. "In any case, I have not found that any variation on the theme of mating is a permanent cure for ideals."

"What do you define as 'ideals'?"

"Irrelevancies, said Byron, "such as truth, love, beauty. And humanity."

"The first three are nonsensical abstractions. The last is a collective noun. No one has agreed on the meanings of any of them, yet they have caused more destruction than the hydrogen wars. That is why, in our city-states we have sacrificed 'ideals' on the altar of stability."

"Assuming that it is better to be a happy pig than an unhappy Socrates?" demanded Byron.

Dr. Krypton shrugged. "Pigs—lamentably now extinct—never had a reasonable happiness quotient. At best they experienced contentment. Socrates, on the other hand, enjoyed himself hugely, if the old accounts are to be believed."

"But happiness consists in adjusting one self to the world. I do not think——"

"On the contrary, you do think, Dr. Byron. But not expertly. Otherwise you would see that only contentment is obtained by adjusting one self to the world—a proposition supported by the extinct pig, which was a creature adequately

11

conditioned to its environment. Conversely, Socrates preferred to adjust the world to himself—and derived the greatest happiness. As you know, he died tranquilly—which is to say, happily. Death, for him, was the final luxury. He was fulfilled."

Dr. Byron looked perplexed. "Perhaps a prefrontal will turn me into a happy Socrates," he said.

Krypton smiled. "Or it may save you from being an unhappy pig. Here is your passport. You will need it because tonight you will visit illiterates block seven, where the girl Thalia doubtless awaits you. One is reluctant to believe that all philosophy derives from sex, but the confirmation is provided daily."

For the first time Byron displayed fear. "What do you know about Thalia?"

"My dear fellow, I warned you that you would have to play without a queen. You came to me yesterday, also, and I gave you deep hypnosis. Believe me, it is less tiring for all concerned. Not only did you tell me all about this Thalia, but you described her charms so minutely that I would have no difficulty in recognizing her in the flesh. She is twenty-three and affects subjective painting. Her H.Q. is about twenty points higher than yours, and her I.Q. about twenty-five lower. Her father was a technician alpha prefrontal, and her mother an illiterate. She is volatile and resilient. Need I say more?"

"What are you going to do about her?" Byron could not keep the anxiety from his voice.

"I am a psychiatrist, not an inquisitor. She is an illiterate. I need take no action."

The younger man was genuinely puzzled. "Why, then, are you allowing me to see her again?"

"I should have thought that was self-evident. By leaving you free to visit her I weaken your resistance. If you take advantage of this final opportunity you will be emotionally exhausted when you come to me tomorrow. If you do not see her you will be frustrated by an unresolved conflict. Either is advantageous, for I shall have to decide what to do with you tomorrow. It will be useful to observe you under stress."

"Why do you tell me this?"

"I can afford to have no secrets. Good morning, Dr. Byron. Here, you are forgetting your passport!"

"Will he give you a prefrontal?" she asked quietly.

They were walking hand in hand through the few acres

of carefully designed woodland between block seven and block eight. Lights, shining from the uncurtained windows of flats, appeared to dance between the leaves of birch, oak and sycamore. Here and there, in symmetrical grassy hollows, illiterates male lay with illiterates female, transforming the mechanics of coition into an old subjective mystery.

"I expect so," he answered. "There is no other solution."

"We could run away," she said. "We could try to reach the primitives in the highlands. They say there are several thousand of them north of the Grampians."

He shook his head. "The co-ordinators would allow an illiterate to escape, but not a technician. Besides, we can't even be sure that the primitives exist."

"Are you afraid?" asked Thalia.

"Yes, for both of us. It will be better when I am sent to the reservation. Then we shall be able to meet frequently."

She gripped his hand tightly. "After the operation, you may not love me any more."

"You can teach me all over again."

"I—I may not want to. You'll feel different about things. With the prefrontals, nothing matters deeply. You'll get bored, and make love to some prefrontal woman, and won't be able to understand how I feel about it."

He stopped, put his arm round her and whispered: "Look at the stars. They're the memory patterns of the cosmos. They are patterns of inconceivable purpose on the brain of space. To them, Nova Mancunia is nothing. It is not even the characteristic of a diseased astrospore! The constellations are outside our time. They shone with the same brilliance when Lake Manchester was a teeming city. They will continue to shine when Nova Mancunia is a more doubtful legend than Troy."

"I'm not sure I understand," she said slowly. "But when you talk like that I want to believe without understanding."

"Do the stars," he asked, "seem still and tranquil?"

"When we look at them together," she answered, "I begin to think we might borrow their stillness."

She heard him laugh softly. "They are hurtling by at millions of kilometers an hour," he said. "They are burning themselves to death to illuminate a journey without destination. They are racing headlong to extinction, or else they are the only still points in a whirlpool of space. Which is it?"

"I don't know."

"Neither do I; and that, my darling, is the greatest secret

13

in the world. Just as they might be dying by the trillion, so we might expand one moment of life into eternity."

Slowly, insistently, he pulled her down into the grassy hollow where they stood. Down through a tunnel of darkness to the oldest innocence of all. Presently, in its own compelling ritual, love became a communicable experience of death.

There they lay, a technician beta male and an illiterate female; each, in a different fashion, awaiting the slow metabolism of resurrection.

Dr. Krypton stared absently through his office window at the deputy director's glass windmill. The enigma remained. Some day, perhaps, the sails would cease to turn, and the passport of a co-ordinator alpha would lie on the psychiatrist's desk.

Revolution or evolution? It seemed to be the peculiar genius of twenty-fifth-century man to be an enemy of both.

The psychiatrist heard the door open and said, without turning around: "Good morning, Dr. Byron. If one and a half squirrels ate one and a half nuts in one and a half minutes, how many nuts would nine squirrels eat in nine minutes?"

"Fifty-four," said Byron, after a short pause.

"Three seconds," observed Krypton. "You are moderately alert. . . . I trust you achieved catharsis last night?"

"I did. I killed her!"

Dr. Krypton turned to face his visitor. "That is interesting. Why did you not kill yourself also?"

"Because I needed to live in order to kill you."

"You are probably stronger than I am," said the psychiatrist calmly. "It appears that Nova Mancunia will presently need a new co-ordinator alpha. And neurosurgeons are difficult to replace. Unfortunately, Dr. Byron, you cannot kill the system."

"I can try."

"You can fail. That is all. Now you had better begin your failure by killing me."

Byron moved forward, then suddenly stopped. He moved forward again, then stopped. His whole body was trembling. Beads of sweat broke out on his forehead.

"I am afraid," said the psychiatrist, "that I took advantage of the deep hypnosis to rearrange, temporarily, your pattern of compulsion and tabu. As you see, it was quite justified. If you can lay a hand on me I assure you there will be no

14

resistance. I have considered your case since yesterday. There does not seem to be any alternative to a prefrontal luecotomy —officially."

"And unofficially?" asked Byron, staring at him dully.

"I shall operate on you, Dr. Byron, but I shall merely make an incision, then close it. There will be no severance of brain fiber."

"Why?"

"Because, my dear fellow, the human race needs you. Until that need is manifest, you will live in the prefrontal reservation."

"One of us is quite mad," said Byron slowly.

"I am," admitted Krypton. "It is incurable. You see, I too have no faith in Nova Mancunia. The present society is not static, and there will come a time when it will fail. That will be the signal for a return to humanity."

"Did you make me kill her?" demanded Byron abruptly.

"I did. You, perhaps, will need to die before a new society is established. I have merely made it easier for you."

For a minute Dr. Byron remained silent. When he spoke his voice was quiet, his manner calm. "When will you operate?"

"Tomorrow morning."

"Are you really not going to cut the fiber, or is that suggestion part of the treatment?"

Dr. Krypton smiled as he ushered his guest out. "It is an interesting point, because you will never know."

> Tomorrow's gift of joy or pain
> renews the problem of desire.
> Behind each vacant pair of eyes
> lurks the sad prisoner of fire.

A QUESTION OF TIME

A thin streak of light curved silently out of the black sky, down toward the almost featureless lava plain and the landing area marked by a wide circle. The rocket hovered for a moment, sitting on its tail of green flame. Then the touchdown shoes made contact, and the flame died.

Presently passengers and crew, wearing combination pressure suits, descended from the entry port by a nylon ladder. The tractor was already waiting for them. When they had settled themselves comfortably in its long pressurized trailer it swung around and headed for a small cluster of plastic bubbles about a mile away.

Five minutes later, over cups of steaming coffee at the spaceport, the passengers were giving their entry permits to the control officer and being routed for ultimate destinations.

Among them was a tall white-haired man whose appearance and age seemed to discredit the photograph and sworn statement on his permit. The control officer was frankly puzzled.

"Just a moment, Professor Reigner. We have your age here as forty-five. Is that—"

"Quite correct," said Otto Reigner with a grim smile. "Anticipating some skepticism, I also brought my birth certificate and a letter of credence. Here they are."

The control officer took the documents and looked at them carefully. They were indisputably genuine, but he was still dissatisfied.

"Is this a recent photograph, sir?"

"It was taken three months ago."

"But you look twenty years younger in it."

"That is so," agreed Reigner calmly, as he replaced the documents in his wallet. He did not seem inclined to offer explanations.

"But—"

"If you think I'm an impostor, I can only advise you to check with Earth. I suggest you contact the Department of Hydroponics, Polar Division."

The control officer looked slightly unhappy. The name Reigner was not entirely unknown in the scientific world, and he had no wish to make a fool of himself.

"Not an impostor, sir," he protested helplessly. "Only it's my duty to see that facts correspond with data."

"Proceed quickly, then," said Reigner. "I have urgent business in Lunar City."

The control officer saw a way out. "With whom, sir?"

"With the Co-ordinator, Starship Research."

"S.S.R.? Excuse me a moment. I'll give them a ring and let them know you're on the way." He turned toward a small office.

The smile on Reigner's face flickered. "They will be quite surprised," he said dryly, "to hear that I'm an old man."

The control officer vanished with an apologetic shrug. A couple of minutes later he emerged from the office looking partly reassured. "They're expecting you, Professor Reigner.

16

There's a moon taxi waiting by the airlock. Will you come this way, please?"

The taxi rocket touched down by the eastern airlock of Lunar City. It had covered the fifty miles from the spaceport in exactly six minutes.

When he stepped out of the airlock Reigner found a courier waiting for him. He was taken down a broad avenue between rows of hiduminium buildings to the administrative headquarters. Presently he was waiting in an anteroom staring at a door marked CO-ORDINATOR STARSHIP RESEARCH, while his courier talked to the man on the other side.

He was not kept waiting long.

Reigner heard the courier being dismissed, then he saw the Co-ordinator's domelike head appear in the doorway.

"Will you come in, Professor?"

He took a seat opposite the Co-ordinator's desk and declined an introductory cigarette. Reigner was subjected to a swift, searching glance and noted at the same time that Co-ordinator Jansen concealed his surprise admirably.

"It is a pleasure to receive such a distinguished biochemist," said Jansen smoothly. "What can I do for you?"

Reigner came straight to the point. "You're probably as busy as I was until it became necessary for me to come and see you. So I won't waste your time. When did you last hear from Star Base Three?"

Jansen raised his eyebrows. "Star Base Three? As a matter of fact, we're expecting a routine call any time. There hasn't been anything for the last three days—which isn't unusual, of course, during a test series. I expect—"

"You've tried to establish contact from this end?" interrupted Reigner.

"Yes, but without urgency. So far as we know there isn't any reason to panic. Copernicus is fifty-six miles wide, and there are installations all around the crater, with only a dozen men—including your brother—to handle the lot. . . . Now what's on your mind?"

Professor Reigner leaned back in his chair wearily. "There isn't any Star Base Three," he said. "Neither is there any starship. . . . Don't ask me how I know. I'll tell you when we've inspected the wreckage."

Jansen was not a man to react slowly. He flipped an intercom switch and gave orders for an inspection rocket to be made available. Then he turned back to Reigner. "What about the personnel?"

17

"Dead," answered Reigner unemotionally. "All of them; I'll show you where the bodies are."

"And your brother?"

"Yes, Max is dead. But we won't find him. . . . Not yet."

The one thing that impressed Jansen was Reigner's utter certainty. Yet the Co-ordinator was aware that this was the first time he had visited the moon, so how could he know about a catastrophe the news of which had not yet reached Lunar City?

Oddly, Jansen didn't doubt the professor for a moment. And suddenly he remembered an interesting fact about the Reigner brothers. They were identical twins.

The Co-ordinator had a sudden mental image of Max Reigner, a tall, dark-haired, vigorous man who looked as if he might still be on the right side of forty. Then he stared incredulously at the man on the other side of his desk—the man with white hair and wrinkled face; tall, certainly, but like a dry stick.

Otto Reigner seemed to divine his thoughts. "Three days ago," he said, "I was twenty years younger. I'll tell you about that, too. But later."

A voice came over the Co-ordinator's intercom. "Inspection rocket standing by, sir."

"Thank you." It suddenly occurred to Jansen that he was not being very hospitable to a man who had traveled two hundred and forty thousand miles to see him. "Would you like to have a rest before we start, Professor? Or a meal, perhaps? Copernicus is about twelve hundred miles from here."

Reigner shook his head. "How long will it take to get there?"

"About forty-five minutes."

"I'm living on coffee and sedatives," said the professor. "Both of which can be taken on the way. That's what comes of jumping twenty years overnight."

The equatorial crater Copernicus was bathed in green earthlight. As he gazed through the visor of his headpiece, while the rocket was still circling at a thousand feet, Professor Reigner was thankful that the green glow toned down the hard contours of the mountains and the desolate rocky flats they encircled.

Jansen spoke to the pilot. "Touch down by the main hutments—what's left of them."

The rocket swooped low, curtsied like a ballerina and sank gracefully on its tail. Jansen was climbing down the ladder almost before the motors had cut out. Reigner followed him clumsily, having not yet adjusted to the weak gravity.

Silently they walked to a small and unmistakably recent crater surrounded by a few twisted girders and metal plates that were torn and crumpled like paper.

Jansen's voice came over his personal radio, taut and strained. "An atomic grenade, by the look of it. But they didn't have any here."

"No, it was a discarded Azimov drive unit," said Reigner. "Max took it from one of the pilot rockets and altered the timing. He wanted to make sure that all records were effectively destroyed."

"I see." The Co-ordinator picked up a strip of metal and examined it. "What do you know about the Azimov star drive?"

'Only what Max told me."

"Much?"

"Not enough to be any use, I'm afraid. My line is bio-chemistry, not sub-space physics."

Jansen walked slowly round the miniature crater, gazing at it with intense concentration. Reigner kept pace with him.

"Do you think he was insane?" asked the Co-ordinator suddenly.

"Give me an objective definition of insanity, and I'll tell you."

Jansen's voice sounded very quiet, as if he were talking to himself: "Five years is too long. Nobody does a five-year tour and gets away with it. But the damn fool wouldn't go back to Earth—not even for a couple of months. Claimed he was always on the point of getting a plus two transition. . . . And this is how it ends."

"It ended with a plus ten transition," said Reigner calmly. "He would have got more, but the transponder died. He realized then that Azimov, when he built the original unit, must never have considered the full implications of beating the light barrier. According to Max, Azimov was merely hoping for a drive that would take men out to the stars within the space of a single lifetime. He would have been satisfied with a safe minus transition of point five. Apparently it didn't occur to him that if you could actually get into the plus range, the way was open for an indefinite series. When Max got plus ten it dawned on him that the interval of transition might be extended until it became instantaneous at infinity —until, in fact, signals came back from all parts of the cosmos simultaneously. That way, a starship could hop around

19

the galaxies—literally in no time at all."

"Ten times faster than light!" exclaimed Jansen. "Dammit, he must have been insane! Assuming he got it, what in hell is the use of it? What could you experience at ten light-years per year?"

"Absolute duration," said Reigner. "It can only be described as a directed stillness. In effect, you would fall through the fabric of space until you hit a previously set deceleration point. As you slowed down to the speed of light you would emerge in space-time again. You would re-enter the world of reality as it appears to those who exist at sub-light velocities. In the process of re-entering, you might achieve orientation—you might, in fact, select the star pattern you want and use its sub-light velocity as a kind of crash barrier. The effect would be like a rocket being slowed down by dense atmosphere—only in this case the atmosphere would be a series of elector-magnetic fields. Anyway, that was Max's theory. And he proved it."

Jansen's features were pretty well hidden by his headpiece, but his voice quivered with excitement. "He could only prove it by making a star journey, and even if he tried for Proxima Centauri he couldn't bring back the proof for nearly a year. Unless the transition was more than ten plus."

Professor Reigner was silent for a few moments. Then he said, "The round trip to Procyon is, I believe, twenty-one light-years. Figure out the transition ratio if it could be accomplished in four days."

"Are you suggesting that—"

"I'm sorry to play the mystery man, Co-ordinator; but I had to show you that Base Three is destroyed and that there isn't any starship before I could hope to make you accept my explanation. The truth is too fantastic to stand without evidence."

Jansen stared at the wrecked installations. "I'd be surprised if the truth wasn't fantastic," he said dryly. "Incidentally, where are the bodies?"

Reigner pointed. A quarter of a mile away, standing near the remains of a living-unit, was a lunar tractor.

"They knew too much. They helped bring the Azimov drive to perfection. They saw it reach a ten plus transition on the pilot rocket. So Max killed them."

"In God's name, why?"

"You yourself suggested insanity, but it is not quite so simple. For five years Max never considered the implications of success. Then, when the theory became fact, when he had

20

it in his power to give humanity the means of conquering interstellar space—of dominating the galaxy, even—he suddenly realized that man was not yet ready to face such tremendous possibilities. Unfortunately the Azimov drive wasn't his secret alone. If he destroyed the starship and pilot rockets, there still remained men who could build others. That is why he killed them."

While Reigner was speaking they had begun to walk toward the tractor.

"It still fits my definition of insanity," said the Co-ordinator grimly. "By himself a man can't make decisions like that. He can't set himself up as a supreme judge to decide what's good for the whole human race. . . . You mentioned Procyon. Am I to understand that he took the ship for a test voyage? It doesn't make sense."

"The last proof," said Reigner. "Whatever else he was still the scientist. He had to know beyond any shadow of doubt that man could survive the transition—and that he hadn't murdered his colleagues in vain."

"*He* had to know," growled Jansen angrily. "The rest of us don't matter a damn."

"Not quite," retorted the professor "Max took a witness, one who might have a good chance of survival. He didn't want to leave you with an unsolved mystery on your hands."

"Who did he take?"

"Me," said Professor Reigner.

They had reached the tractor. Eleven bodies had been neatly stacked inside its pressurized compartment But the airlock was open. Jansen scrambled through it and examined the dead men. There were no signs of violence at all.

"It is expedient that eleven men shall die to save humanity." His voice was bitter. "Even if that were so, I don't think these boys would have appreciated the historical perspective. How did he do it?"

Reigner gazed at the corpses somberly. "Carbon monoxide. It was before we became *en rapport*. There would have been no suffering."

Jansen came out of the tractor, closing the airlock behind him. He gave the professor a searching look. But earthlight, glinting on the vizor of his headpiece, effectively screened Reigner's expression

"Let's get this straight, Professor. You've never been to the moon before, yet you took a test voyage on a ship using the Azimov drive. You were never at Base Three, yet you know all about its destruction. Your age is forty-five, yet you look more than sixty. I think the time has come to fill in a few minor details."

Reigner's grim laughter came over his personal radio like a harsh croaking. "There's one other thing, Co-ordinator. The starship is due back in about twenty hours. It has been programed to crash here in Copernicus."

Jansen was getting beyond surprise. "Naturally it's going to crash—otherwise, we'd have the perfected Azimov drive. But why pick on Copernicus? Why should it come back here?"

Reigner spoke slowly. "Can you imagine how lonely it is to die among the stars? Max wasn't altogether ruthless, you know. Those men he killed, they were his friends, the men with whom he worked and whose world he shared. This would be his way of coming back to them, of making the same sacrifice. Who knows? It may be his way of reporting success."

"Insane," said the Co-ordinator flatly. "It's the only possible explanation. . . . And now you'd better tell me all about it, right from the beginning."

"It's quite a long story. If there's any coffee left on board the rocket, I think I could use some. And you might as well listen in comfort."

The two men turned around and tramped slowly back over the dusty, barren rockface toward the inspection rocket. Their footsteps superimposed on the startlingly fresh tracks of men who were already dead, and of one whose distance away could only be measured in light-years.

Presently they reached the rocket and climbed the ladder. And with even intensity, green earthlight poured down upon the crater Copernicus—a great bowl of desolation with here and there a few fragments of twisted metal as evidence of an already petrified tragedy. And, circling the entire lake of dusty rock, a ring of saw-toothed uneroded mountains, heavy with the secrets of a billion years.

Max Reigner and Haggerty, the electronics rigger, were in the radio room waiting for firing point, filling in the time with a fateful and classic argument. Outside the lab unit, three miles away, the experimental rocket threw its long slender shadow across the crater floor. The sun was already low over the mountains. In another few hours the harsh contours of Copernicus would soften under a green twilight. But by that time Pilot 7 Mark III would no longer stand glowing like a fat metallic cigar in the barren crater. It would already have passed out of sub-light existence and be cruising at a radiation-plus velocity through unimaginable stretches of galactic desert. Or else, having failed to pass the light barrier, it would be nothing more than a thin skein of vapor drifting with snail-like certainty toward some hungry star.

Max Reigner had great hopes for Pilot 7. The Mark III Azimov unit had been rebuilt and reoriented from diamond pivots to oscillator, and Haggerty's work on the deuteron discharge had increased its efficiency to 93 per cent. But chiefly he was optimistic because intuition told him that there could be no more improvements to make, and that now there remained but two simple possibilities. Either he would get a plus transition increasing until the transponder failed, or else he would know finally that the Azimov technique was a waste of time. And after five years of hard work rewarded only by failure, Max Reigner still had faith in the Azimov drive. Now that the bugs had been shaken out of it, now that the deuteron efficiency had been stepped up, there could only be one result. . . .

He stared impatiently at the vision screen, at the fiery silhouette of Pilot 7. In another twenty minutes it would dissolve into a blazing arc. He began to fret about the radiostroboscope and wonder how long the transponder would hold out, and at the same time he tried to listen to what Haggerty was saying.

The electronics rigger was developing his favorite theme. "So you've got to have conflict. It isn't love, it isn't money what makes the world go round. It's just good old-fashioned club-him-and grab-it conflict. Take the dinosaur; take Neanderthal man; take the civilizations of Egypt, Greece and Rome. What made them fold? What made them pack up and walk right out of history? Nothing but sweet, simple conflict. Or let's give it a nice physical basis. Let's call it friction. Sooner or later they rubbed up against something that was harder than they were. So they got rubbed out. It's the basic law, Max. Man against odds, civilization against odds, species against odds. The whole damn cosmos is a conspiracy organized against every single living thing. And once you get the idea that you're civilized enough to get along without relying on that primitive dynamism, without scalping the other fellow before he scalps you, you might as well sit down and write your will. Because you're decadent. That's what's wrong with Earth now. The whole planet has gone soft. You know what it needs to pump back that lost virility?"

Max Reigner stared at the image of Pilot 7, and ran a hand through his dark hair. He said dryly, "I have my own misguided ideas but I might as well hear yours."

"The Azimov drive," announced Hagerty, "with a transition of a hundred plus."

"Tell me more. If we're all saviors here we might as well know it."

"Take the years out of light-years," explained Haggerty, tossing himself a cigarette, "and what are we going to get? Starships. Hundreds of 'em. Fleets of 'em. Cruising around the galaxy looking for plums. Like the Romans when they got their teeth into Africa, or the Spaniards when they stepped ashore in Mexico, or the British in India. We're going to hit a new age of empire building. The solar system versus the rest. Can't you see it, a hundred years from now, the solar empire with maybe fifty habitable planets under our control? That's the kind of challenge to put the guts back into humanity. And here are we, all set to trigger a new deal in history. If that Mark III unit does the trick we'll make Cortez, Alexander and the rest look like juvenile delinquents."

"If I thought so," said Reigner coldly, "I'd wreck the experimental rockets right now. And I'd make it my business to break up every other star project. The trouble with you, Haggerty, is that you're just a goddamned anachronism. Your ugly little jungle mind slobbers for power and possession."

"We're in the cosmic jungle," grinned Haggerty. "Got to look for coconuts and watch out for tigers."

"We're in the cosmic laboratory," retorted Reigner. "We're here to make experiments and to investigate—not to spend our time grabbing test tubes from each other."

Hagerty's amusement increased. "You be the scientist, I'll be the gorilla. History's on my side. What happens to every nice invention served up by the gentlemen scientists? The gorillas grab it for their own use from arrowheads to atomic disintegration, from windmills to solar power. They'll grab the Azimov drive, too. Pretty soon there'll be shiploads of educated gorillas drifting around the stars, using atomics, ultrasonics, therm jets and what-have-you to peel their celestial bananas. Who knows, maybe I'll be out there myself—staking out a million acres on Planet X, or organizing a squad of three-legged coolies."

Max Reigner glanced at the clock, then twisted the screen controls to get a sharper outline of Pilot 7. A voice came over the wallspeaker: "Five minutes to firing point."

The physicist looked thoughtfully at Haggerty. "You're a third-rate cynic and a first-rate fool. If you read any history

24

at all you'd realize that the sort of piracy you seem to admire damn near finished off the planet—until science forced the grab-it boys to co-operate or die. And now you want to start the same kind of free-for-all again on a cosmic scale. Don't you people ever learn? Doesn't it occur to you that sooner or later the grab-type is bound to grab something that's too big for him to handle? And what happens if you go out to the stars and find other educated gorillas with a better science behind them? You take them on, I suppose, until they find your home planet and do a spot of colonizing themselves. Or destroy it."

"Three minutes to firing point," said the wall-speaker.

Haggerty blew a cloud of smoke and stubbed out his cigarette. "Survival of the fittest," he said. "If they're strong enough to lick us, good luck to 'em. The law of the cosmic jungle."

"Cosmic lunacy! You're emotionally retarded. You think of a starship as a galactic privateer. To me it's a survey ship—a means of getting out and looking, not getting out and taking. Before I'd present the successful star drive to a bunch of trigger-happy pirates I'd either destroy it or them. Now stop blathering and wrap yourself around that box of tricks. I want a dead accurate strobograph."

"Here's to it," remarked Haggerty, glancing at Pilot 7. "Prototype Santa Maria—star version. . . . You know, I like you, Max. You're a magnificent paradox. You think you're just a peaceful scientist, but in your heart you're as homicidal as the rest of us. Only difference is, you'd kill for ideas not things."

"One minute to firing point," said the wallspeaker. "Forty-five seconds . . . thirty seconds . . . fifteen seconds . . . ten, nine, eight, seven, six, five, four, three, two, one—zero!"

On the vision screen there was a sudden brightness as the volatility rocket lifted Pilot 7 out of Copernicus. In a few more minutes, when it was clear of the moon's G field, the booster could cut in. Then when that died the Azimov unit would come into action. Already the transponder was pinging at one-second intervals.

Max Reigner watched the experimental rocket swing silently up as if lifted on the rim of an invisible wheel. Up past the mountains in a bright blaze of sunlight.

There was nothing more to be seen. He turned to the transponder and waited. It continued pinging evenly and the figures began to come out on a thin strip of paper. He looked at Haggerty, hunched over the radio-stroboscope like a giant spider, fingers delicately adjusting the range control, eyes fixed on the swinging red needle, while the pattern of oscillations was graphed by an automatic stylo.

One thought began to repeat itself insistently in Reigner's tense mind: "Gorillas grab . . . gorillas grab . . . gorillas grab . . ." It became meaningless—a hypnotic incantation.

He looked at the figures coming out of the transponder. 1.00 . . . 1.00 . . . 1.00 . . . 1.00 . . . 1.00 . . . 1.00 . . . 1.01 . . . 1.01 . . .

Reigner fancied he could detect the slightly different interval, that he could appreciate audibly the difference of a hundredth of a second. 1.01 . . . 1.01 . . . 1.02 . . . 1.02 . . .

As soon as the figures had begun to change he knew that the Azimov unit was operating. There would be a steep climb, now, as Pilot 7 plowed into the close sub-light velocities. Or else there would be an eloquent silence. The last experimental ship had blown itself out of existence at 1.70. At more than a hundred thousand miles a second in terms of a space-time block which it could not physically occupy.

The idea of the velocity check was elegantly simple. Pilot 7 produced pinger signals at the rate of one every second. If eventually those signals were received at one every two seconds it would mean that the ship had achieved threshold velocity—that is, the speed of light. Any subsequent increase in interval would show that the light barrier had been passed and that total submersion in space had been achieved. At which point, theoretically, there would be no further physical crises—and there would be nothing to stop Pilot 7 stepping up to an infinite velocity.

"Gorillas grab . . . gorillas grab . . . gorillas grab," thought Reigner mechanically. And then he heard the pinger signals change to a lower note. The difference in interval was apparent. The numbers on the paper roll were increasing quickly.

1.20 . . . 1.25 . . . 1.31 . . . 138 . . . 1.46 . . . 1.54 . . . 1.64 . . .

"Gorillas grab . . . gorillas grab . . . gorillas grab . . ." There was sweat on Reigner's forehead. His hands were shaking so much he could scarcely hold the strip of paper steady. The figures began to dance before his eyes—a rhythmic jungle dance.

"Christ, we've passed it!" croaked Haggerty. The red needle gave a violent lurch, then remained steady. The graph stopped looking like a mountain range and became a smooth parabola.

1.75 . . . 1.86 . . . 1.98 . . . Pilot 7 was passing 180,000 miles per second. Then the pinger hit the two-second interval. There was a faint suggestion of hesitation, a sudden change of note. Haggerty flung an awestruck glance at his chief, and at the same time the radio-stroboscope went dead.

But still the numbers came out of the transponder.

2.21 . . . 2.35 . . . 2.54 . . . 2.66 . . .

"Light!" roared Haggerty. "By God, we've licked it. We've knocked it silly!"

"Listen to the pinger," snapped the physicist. "It's beginning to throb!" And still that damned incantation, picking up the rhythm of the pinger. "Gorillas grab . . . gorillas grab . . . gorillas grab . . ."

2.83 . . . 3.01 . . . 3.20 . . . 3.40 . . . 3.61 . . . 3.83 . . . 4.07 . . .

"Six hundred thousand miles a second!" gasped Haggerty. "Godalmighty! We'll hit the million!"

"Quiet, you bloody fool!" Reigner's voice was high-pitched, breaking.

4.32 . . . 4.58 . . . 4.85 . . . 5.13 . . . 5.42 . . . 5.72 . . . 6.03 . . . 6.35 . . . 6.68 . . . 7.02 . . . 7.37 . . . 7.75 . . . 8.14 . . . 8.54 . . . 8.95 . . . 9.37 . . . 9.80 . . . 10.24 . . . 10.69 . . . 11.15 . . . Silence. The pinger broke off in mid-moan. The transponder died.

White-faced, Reigner collapsed in his chair, not trusting himself to speak

"A transition of ten plus," whispered Haggerty. "Two million miles a second. Goddamnit, two million crazy miles a second! Gimme some wings and call me an angel. By God, we've knocked a hole clean through space. Ten years from now we'll have a fleet of 'em—buzzing around the galaxy." His voice rose gaily. "Up the old solar empire—and three cheers for the gentlemen scientists!"

Reigner said nothing. He sat hunched in his chair, staring ahead with unseeing eyes. But in imagination there was the vision of Pilot 7 coursing swiftly through the sub-dimensional void. And sitting astride it, wearing an inane toothy grin, was a barrel-chested gorilla.

Presently others came into the radio room. They looked at Reigner curiously, then listened to Haggerty's highly dramatic account of the transition build-up and its technical implications. And after a time Reigner came back to life. He listened to congratulations; he allowed his hand to be shaken, his back to be slapped; he registered a vague smile and mumbled words that had no meaning for him.

27

He realized dimly that he was being taken to the living-unit, that bottles were being opened, that toasts were being drunk. Then Haggerty, with an ironic gleam in his eye, called on him to make a formal speech.

Reigner pulled himself together and began to talk. And as he talked his gaze wandered round the circle of well-known faces. He seemed to be looking for something—something he knew he would never find.

The men of Star Base Three, looking at their chief, saw in the strange brilliance of his eyes a vision of solar expansion, the dream of a space-born civilization bridging the star-gaps —perhaps, even, in the final stage a unified segment of the galaxy controlled by the benevolent despots of Earth. All this and more would be possible with starships using the perfected Azimov drive, and manned by explorers intent on "pacifying" other life forms on other planets in the name of progress.

But Reigner's eyes were only bright with tears. There would be no great star-rush, no celestial Klondike, no stampede of educated gorillas to slake their Earthborn avarice on distant worlds.

He looked sadly at that small circle of men—men who had worked with him for months, in some cases years, on the Azimov unit. Men who had shared his faith. The men who would have to die.

Reigner cursed himself silently for being a scientist first and a human being second; for being a specialist and therefore only a clever idiot; for concentrating on means and forgetting all about ends. For failing to realize that humanity was still just a gawky adolescent.

As soon as he could he escaped from the general celebrations and made his way to the dormitory. He lay down on his bunk, closed his eyes and tried to relax. But sleep, when it came, brought no relief—only the dream symbolism of what he needed to forget.

Reigner awoke when everyone else had turned in. He switched on his bunk light and saw that he had been asleep six hours. The reality of his achievement—for, basically, the success belonged to him—came flooding back. And with it, knowledge of the consequences.

He wanted to delay, but there was no need to delay. There was no excuse. In fact, if it was to be done at all, it would have to be done quickly. Already, he should have contacted Co-ordinator Jansen at Lunar City and given him the results. Pretty soon the silence at Star Base Three would make Lunar City anxious. They would send someone out.

Nor did the starship itself present any excuse for delay. It had sat patiently on its tail in the desolate crater for more than fifteen years—ever since Conrad Azimov had taken the sister-ship on a voyage that had ended in silence. Reigner knew why Azimov had never returned. The ship had vaporized long before it even reached the transition range. But now the original unit had been replaced by a Mark III—identical with the one that had successfully operated in Pilot 7. It only remained for him to climb aboard, close the entry-port and start the take-off motor.

Reviewing the situation as he lay in his bunk in the semi-darkness, Max Reigner became suddenly calm—calmer than he had ever been. He listened to the quiet, steady breathing of the others and formulated his plan of action.

After a time he got up noiselessly and tiptoed to the door. In the anteroom, he put on a pressure suit then went toward the airlock.

A few seconds later he stepped outside the living unit and was alone under the black star-riddled sky. The sun had totally disappeared, leaving only dull green earthlight that gave the mountains of Copernicus an odd illusion of movement during the long lunar darkness.

Reigner stared at the stars for a moment or two, then began to walk briskly over the rocky floor, heading for the chemilab. Presently he returned with two gas cylinders on a small trolley. He took them to the dormitory airlock and dumped them, one at a time, in the pressure chamber. Then he closed the outer door, raised the pressure and finally took off his headpiece so that he would be able to hear.

Cautiously he maneuvered each cylinder into the dormitory. He stood still, listening, until he was satisfied that no one was awake. Then he unscrewed the taps. The hiss of escaping carbon monoxide seemed to him like the roar of terrestrial rapids, but no one stirred. After a couple of minutes he went out, closing the door quietly behind him.

For the next few hours Max Reigner pursued the grim work of demolition with tremendous energy, giving himself hardly any time to rest and no time at all to think. Everything in Copernicus must be destroyed—with the exception of the starship. All records of the Azimov technique and the painstaking research which had led to its perfection would be obliterated forever.

He took a personnel tractor and set out across the crater on his wrecking tour. At each laboratory, each workshop, each storechamber, he used whatever materials came to hand— volatility fuels, solid explosives, old rocket motors and even a couple of Mark II Azimov units. At the powerhouse, he smashed the governors on the atomic engine, and even as he drove away the whole plant shot silently skyward in a great gout of flame.

Eventually there was only one group of buildings left— the dormitory and the living-unit. He swung the tractor around and headed back across the crater, driving crazily at full speed over the unyielding rock. The tour of destruction had already taken him more than a hundred miles.

Presently the starship loomed on the horizon—a tall slender column pointing ominously up toward the great star-gaps. He drove past it without stopping. There was yet the final act of destruction before he could make that fateful voyage—before he could make the ultimate test of the Azimov drive and see whether a human being could survive the transition.

A thought suddenly struck him. Suppose he had killed in vain! Suppose it was impossible for living tissue to survive the big jump! Suppose the stars could never have been menaced by boatloads of educated gorillas anyway!

But in his heart Reigner did not believe in failure, could not even accept it as possible. The star-flight would doubtless be traumatic; but man had learned to face trauma, had managed to survive the greatest trauma of all—birth. This, too, might be a kind of birth.

The tractor stopped. Reigner saw that his own hand had switched off the engine. With surprise he realized that he was back at the dormitory. He jumped down from the tractor and went to the airlock. As he passed through he automatically took off his headpiece.

There was no sound of breathing now. No deadly hiss of carbon monoxide. The cylinders were empty. The bodies lay quite still in their bunks. Reigner felt a warning heaviness, swayed a little and hastily put on his headpiece again. Then he tried to switch on the main light, and only when it didn't work did he remember that he had blown up the powerhouse. He unhooked the torch from his belt and went around to inspect the dead.

No signs of stress. They were peaceful enough. They might still have been sleeping. He looked at Haggerty—eyes closed, lips closed, but still wearing that damnable smile.

Reigner had meant to destroy everything, but he could

not bring himself to destroy the bodies. As he took them out to the tractor, one by one, he wondered what his motive might be.

They were dead, and nothing worse could happen to them. It wouldn't matter to them whether their bodies were blown to bits or preserved like mummies in the lunar vacuum. He tried to remember whether he had ever believed in ghosts.

At last the work of demolition was completed. With the wrecking of the dormitory and living-unit, Star Base Three was completely razed to the ground. All that remained of an experimental station founded on the proposition that mankind shall reach the stars were a couple of tractors, eleven bodies, a starship and a man who had chosen the most elaborate method of committing suicide ever devised.

Presently there would be only the tractors and the bodies, wrapped in an impregnable cocoon of silence.

Max Reigner began to walk toward the starship. It was quite a distance and he could have taken a tractor. But he preferred to walk. He wanted to feel the hard ground under his feet. Above all, he would have given anything—if there had been anything left to give—to take off his headpiece and breathe once more the living air of Earth. As he walked he glanced at the green-tinted lava beds, the green mountains of Copernicus; and tried to clothe their sharp contours in his imagination with grass and trees, and the now almost forgotten beauty of rivers.

He arrived at the ship too soon, knowing that it would always have been too soon. As he climbed aboard he began to wonder how long it would take the two remaining star bases on the moon to catch up with the Azimov project.

Twenty years? Fifty? A hundred? It was hard to say, because they had different lines of approach. They were still working on atomic methods. No one but Max Reigner had had sufficient faith in the Azimov technique to waste his time on the whys and wherefores of an incomprehensible transition. The mathematicians laughed and said it was theoretically possible, *but* . . . The conventional physicists merely shrugged.

Conrad Azimov had been mad; and so, apparently, was Max Reigner. If he wanted to chase a shadow they wouldn't stop him; but neither would they help him. Which was one of the reasons why there had been only eleven assistants at Base Three when the other bases had a complement of fifty. The Administration could afford to lose a certain amount of money, but not too much.

Closing the entry-port behind him, finally cutting himself off from the world that understood too little and always knew too much, Reigner concluded that it might well be a hundred years before human beings could successfully bridge the star-gaps.

Long enough for the educated gorillas to drop the grab game? He didn't know. He could only hope.

He went up to the navigation deck, took out a star-map, closed his eyes and put a finger down. Procyon. A near star. He was irrationally glad.

The time it took him, working with computer and auto-pilot, to get the programing equations out was meaningless. At the end of it all his knees gave way, and he diagnosed hunger.

He made his way to the mess-deck and got some food together which he ate sitting by an observation frame and staring fixedly at the gray-green shadows of Copernicus. He didn't seem to be able to taste the food at all, but presently the hunger pains died down. And that was sufficient.

Eventually he went back to the navigation deck and lay down on the contour-berth by the main panel. He gazed at the bank of illuminated instruments for a few seconds, then he selected a red switch and pressed it firmly. The volatility motors shuddered into life.

He had expected transition to be a kind of icy bubble of darkness, or a maelstrom that would drain him of all sensation. He had thought that sub-spatial existence would involve the negation of all feeling, even of all perception. He was wrong.

Transition was the cosmic parallel of dawn—a gray light intensifying, permeating the whole starship, emanating from the very molecules that, in by-passing the light barrier, had surrendered their own reality and become mere shadows of an organized energy pattern.

Transition was a ripple, a strange shimmering—like the disturbed reflections in a pool. It was a rhythmic stillness, a dance of immobility, the calm waters under a swelling sea of light-years.

Transition was a chord of memory and, above all, it was the absolute loneliness. The long vista of remembered dreams.

The starship, a shell without substance, a hurtling citadel of stillness, had passed clean through the mirror of space-time. The only continuum, now, was a bright gray dawn, a lack of movement in the smooth fall to existence.

Reigner was drowning. The gray torrent swirled about him, rocking every fragment of his life in the suddenly sharp kaleidoscope of memory.

And dominating the succession of tableaux—the mirage of childhood, the oddly vivid fictions of Earth life—was the face of a familiar stranger.

His own reflection? No. There was a subtle difference. A vague confusion. The mystery tormented him until, with a sense of shock, he realized it was the face of his brother.

It was the first time he had thought of Otto since Pilot 7 had risen from Copernicus. In all his thoughts, in all his calculations, Otto had been a blind spot.

But now the face became clearer, more real. Even more real than himself. It was as if he, Max, had begun to fade in proportion to Otto's increasing reality. As if he, the starship and even transition itself had become nothing more than a dream, stretching back through the light barrier into a world of space-time; and through that, through an ultra-dimensional realm of telekinetics or E.S.P. to the receptive darkness of another mind.

Dimly Max tried to recall the psychological theory of empathy—*einfuhlung*—in relation to twins and super-twins. But the effort was too much. It obtruded on Otto's growing reality. It was not a thing to examine too closely in a preternatural dawn-light.

So he waited, trying not to believe that he would drown. Trying to convince himself that the gray torrent of dawn, the whirlpool of isolation, would eventually subside.

And, goaded by the absolute loneliness of transition, he reached out desperately for companionship, projected a living dream, projected a witness into the first star voyage. . . .

Co-ordinator Jansen stared at the man opposite him calmly sipping his coffee. "And you claim it was merely a question of becoming *en rapport?*"

"I did not use the word 'merely,' " said Otto Reigner. He hesitated. "Think of it as a kind of resonance, not limited by time or space."

"Damn it, the starship wasn't in time or space," retorted Jansen irritably. "Are you trying to tell me that this kind of E.S.P. can operate on a sub-spatial level?"

"Why not?" said Professor Reigner. "Take precognition, for example. It is an established scientific fact. People endowed with the faculty have been able to predict future events under laboratory conditions. Now where is the event at the time of prediction? It is not in space, nor is it in time. It has yet to emerge."

"From sub-space?" demanded Jansen with skepticism.

"Possibly; I don't know. I'm only pointing out that it must have some condition of existence on a level that we can't normally perceive."

The Co-ordinator stared moodily out of the rocket's observation dome as if, in some way, the mute rocks of Copernicus would confirm or deny this fantastic explanation.

At last he said, "There's no point in wasting our time here. We'd better get back to Lunar City. You can tell me the rest on the way."

"What about the starship's return?" asked the professor.

A thin smile played on Jansen's lips. "In about twenty hours, I think you said. Very well, we'll be here to meet it—just in case it doesn't crash. Why are you so sure it is going to return?"

"Because I assisted with the programing," said the professor wearily.

The Co-ordinator shrugged. He talked to the pilot over the intercom and gave him his instructions. Then he turned to Professor Reigner. "You can tell me the rest when we level off. Take it up from the point where you became involved. This psychic stuff is a big pill to swallow. You appreciate that, don't you?"

"None better," came the dry answer. "As you see, it has aged me considerably."

A subdued vibration signaled the rocket's smooth rise. Copernicus dropped quickly away. Looking through the vision panel, the professor saw only a swinging pattern of stars. He felt unreasonably cold and began to shiver.

Theatre Five at Byrd University in the International Zone of Antarctica was filled to capacity. Professor Otto Reigner had just begun his introductory lecture.

His youthful figure contrasted oddly with a grave and occasionally pompous way of speaking, and it was not always easy to remember him as the man chiefly responsible for transforming Antarctica into one of the great food-producing areas of the world.

The audience—mainly young engineers, biochemists and doctors—listened with dutiful attention.

"With a population of four thousand million," the professor

was saying, "it would be foolish of us to expect the soil of this planet to supply our needs adequately and indefinitely. You are all aware of the popular hostility to hydroponics. We need not go into that now." He paused. He appeared to stagger, and suddenly clutched his chest.

The audience leaned forward expectantly. There were stifled exclamations and sly, whispered remarks about hang-overs. But the professor, quickly recovering himself, continued as if nothing had happened, and the audience settled down.

"It is sufficient for me to mention that a great propaganda and educational campaign is steadily disposing of the current nonsense and suspicion." Another pause. Reigner swayed drunkenly and grabbed at a chair for support.

A low murmur swept around the theatre. A few people at the front stood up with the vague idea of giving assistance. But again the professor recovered himself quickly, and waved them back with an imperious gesture.

"In any case, the general distrust of hydroponics and other revolutionary methods of food production is of little actual importance. As the population increases we shall discover that hunger is a great destroyer of prejudice. I—I—wish to —to concentrate instead . . . on . . ."

The professor's face was deathly pale. Suddenly he collapsed. Even before he hit the rostrum a doctor leaped toward him.

After a quick examination he was lifted onto an emergency stretcher and carried to a small restroom. Altogether, he remained unconscious for two hours and fifty minutes. The doctors could find nothing wrong on a preliminary examination; all responses were normal.

But while they argued among themselves, and applied the more complex heart and brain tests, a slow and incomprehensible change was taking place.

Reigner's pigmentation was altering. His skin was becoming mottled and flaccid. His dark hair imperceptibly turned dull brownish-gray, then gray, then showed streaks of white. And while most of the medicos seemed to be paralyzed by this incredible acceleration of the aging process, one of the brighter ones made another interesting discovery: Professor Reigner was rapidly losing weight.

Eventually he returned to consciousness. At first he refused to believe that he had been out for less than three hours. But the facts were inescapable.

Professor Reigner took a look at himself in a mirror, gave

a grim smile and said, "Now, gentlemen, will someone kindly register accommodation for me on the next moon rocket?"

They thought he was mad. They wanted to know what it was all about. They tried to work on the connection between a psychosomatic breakdown and a compulsion to go to Lunar City. Professor Reigner did not enlighten them. He merely repeated his request with increasing urgency.

Eventually they capitulated, but tried to get him to take a companion, pointing out that a further attack was possible.

The professor blandly disagreed. There would be no more "attacks," he told them, *because he knew*.

And since his prestige in the scientific world was considerable, and since none of the doctors had the courage to say what they all felt, Professor Reigner got his reservation on the moon rocket.

Even as he traveled to the spaceport the aging process continued.

The gray dawn-light of transition swirled ever brighter through the shimmering starship. The instrument panel, the whole navigation deck, seemed to oscillate slowly between existence and nonexistence. Max Reigner could only wait and hope.

But now there was something more real than the entire star voyage, something that checked a tide of insane laughter almost on the point of effecting its own sinister transition. There was—communication; the transparent shape of Otto Reigner steadily became opaque, steadily clothed itself in the illusion of substance. Watching, fascinated, Max saw the lips move. He heard no sound, but the words flashed clearly in his mind.

And then he felt the thought-stream, the two-way flow of images passing between his own mind and that of his brother.

Otto's pattern resolved itself into dark clouds of bewilderment suddenly pierced by a shoal of questions.

Max transmitted images of Star Base Three; of Pilot 7 rising from Copernicus; of Haggerty's conception of a solar empire; of the figures coming from the transponder; of himself taking the cylinder of carbon monoxide into the dormitory; of his tour of destruction; and of the starship's journey to transition.

Otto's reply signified understanding and a strange pity. Then he flashed a pattern of stars on which a large question mark was superimposed.

Max answered with an image of Procyon.

Otto radiated acceptance. Then he threw a picture of the lecture theatre at the University; of himself on the rostrum; of his sudden collapse.

Max felt anxiety, self-accusation. Otto replied with confidence and curiosity. He walked about the navigation deck, examining the starship, while Max lay on his contourberth—exhausted, but no longer alone. Presently Otto himself lay down on a contourberth and waited expectantly.

With an effort Max glanced at the instrument panel. Everything was still shimmering, still blurred. But he got an impression of the indicator swinging toward deceleration point. And then the gray brightness became unbearable. He closed his eyes, but the brightness seemed to penetrate his body, seemed to drift agonizingly through his brain.

The brightness became a roll of thunder—thunder of light bursting in the starship. Until it seemed as if the sheer mass of radiant energy would break everything apart.

Then suddenly there was nothing but darkness. The strange wave world of transition generated a last tremendous ripple. Then it snapped like a taut wire at breaking point. And there remained only the black infinities of space, the remote tapestry of stars, and a ship that seemed to be the still center of a slowly turning universe.

It was a long time before Max Reigner opened his eyes. Then he got up unsteadily, gazed with disbelief at the now solid contours of the navigation deck, and lurched toward the nearest observation frame.

The constellations had shifted slightly, but the total pattern of the sky was much the same. Without any difficulty he picked out Betelgeux, Aldebaran, Sirius and others.

Dead ahead was a strange sun, white and brilliant. He guessed it to be about twenty light-minutes away, and was elated with a sense of achievement. Even through the darkened plastiglass, its radiance was too intense to be faced. There was no mistaking its identity.

Procyon.

He turned to find Otto standing by his side, and opened his mouth to speak. The words became sounds, filling the starship with their meaning.

"Fantastic," said Co-ordinator Jansen, "utterly fantastic; The devil of it is, I believe you. In fact, I've got to believe you. Otherwise . . ." He tailed off helplessly and gazed at Otto Reigner, still sipping his interminable coffee, as if at any

37

moment he expected him to disappear.

They were in Jansen's private apartment at Lunar City, where the professor was now concluding his story in relative comfort. Even during the short time since his arrival on the moon Professor Reigner seemed to have added a few more years to his appearance. The Co-ordinator began to wonder whether it was just plain fatigue, or whether the "process" was still operating. If the latter, he wondered just how long Reigner could last, how long it would be before senility set in and his mind and body degenerated together.

The professor seemed to divine his thoughts. "Not very long," he said softly. "The stress was too great. My metabolism is already breaking down. That was the second reason why I had to get here quickly."

"What was the first?" asked Jansen hastily.

"I want to see the return. Somehow, that will make the whole thing complete."

The Co-ordinator was silent for a few moments, then he said abruptly; "What about planets? Were there any—or didn't you have time for observation?"

"Two," said the professor. "Max did a rough calculation and said there ought to be at least four. We managed to get the two by manual telescope."

"Close enough for any detail?"

"No. One looked vaguely like Mars, but with more oxygen. Might have been inhabitable, I suppose. Might even have a complex life form of its own."

Jansen couldn't conceal his exasperation. "Why does he have to try and knock history on the head with a crowbar? Why in hell does he have to make decisions for the rest of us?"

"Who—Max? I told you his reasons."

"Not valid. Phoney."

Reigner flashed a faint smile. "But valid for him. When men can understand the motives of individualists like Max they may possibly be fit to make the star voyage. But not, I think, before."

"You agree with him?"

"A little. Only I realize the futility of trying to put a brake on history."

Jansen began to pace up and down. "I suppose it's definite—about the starship crashing, I mean? If only we could collect that Azimov unit!"

Professor Reigner poured himself more coffee. "Even while we were working out the programing for the return journey,

38

Max was already dying. He knew it and I knew it. The whole effort had been to much—not transition itself but the other things. The effort of forcing himself to kill eleven men, of demolishing the star base, and then the final strain of psycho-projection. But in any case, transition isn't the sort of thing to face alone."

"He didn't actually die while you were there?" persisted Jansen.

"That wouldn't have been possible," said the professor. "He was controlling me. How could I have remained projected with a dead control?"

"So you couldn't witness his death?"

"No. By the time we were stepping up to the return transition, Max was too weak to retain me. I just literally faded."

"Then it would be theoretically possible for him to alter the crash programing," remarked the Co-ordinator hopefully.

"Not during transition—and I think that would finish him."

"But afterward, if he survived—"

"*If* he survived," interrupted the professor wearily, "it would be possible. But to what end? Why invalidate his own motives?"

Jansen shrugged. "The logic of the whole thing is beyond my reach, anyway. I'm just indulging in the wistful hope that there's a million-to-one chance."

Otto Reigner stood up and passed a hand over his eyes. For a few moments he didn't seem to be able to focus properly. Then he pulled himself together.

"It's time we went back to Copernicus," he said. "I wouldn't want to be too late."

Darkness was still the darkness of star-gaps, but soon there would be another darkness, impenetrable, unending. . . .

Astern, the white ball of Procyon began to glow a dull red as the starship raced away toward transition. Presently the redness intensified, spreading to other stars and through the constellations. Presently the ship passed smoothly into its approach velocity.

Max Reigner lay helplessly on the contour-berth, keeping his eyes open only by a supreme physical effort. Dully he wondered if he could manage to last until transition.

Already the figure of Otto was wavering, returning to transparency. Soon Max would no longer be able to hold him. Soon the terrible isolation would return—a brief prelude to eternity.

Images tumbled into his mind and he realized that Otto

was using thought-stream to transmit a warning of his imminent departure and to ask if there was anything Max would wish him to do when he got back to Earth—if he got back.

Exerting himself, Max tried to think. There must be some message or decision. But nothing seemed important any more. Nothing that he could remember.

He flashed back a negative, following it with patterns of gratitude and farewell, all mixed crazily with images of childhood, shared adventures in a world of dreamy unreality.

Suddenly Otto transmitted an impression of Lunar City, then an interrogative.

Max had an odd impulse to try to flash the Azimov modifications, then became angry at his weakness, and knew that there was no time, anyway. He threw a safe reply, a noncommittal reply: *Tell them what you know.*

Otto's answer was affirmative. Then he began to build up another image. It remained faint. It refused to take shape in Max's mind. It drifted away, unrecognizable. He waited for Otto to try again. But there was no second attempt.

Vaguely Max peered round the navigation deck. There was nothing to be seen. Only that strange remembered shimmering.

Only the gray dawn-light of transition.

The inspection rocket was circling Copernicus at five thousand feet. Earthlight made the crater bed look like a smooth green lake.

The Co-ordinator's expressionless gaze alternated between the crater and the sky. "This is the fourteenth circuit," he said. "No starship. If there's a time error, what do you think would be the probable magnitude?"

Professor Reigner ignored the question. "It will come," he said.

But Jansen didn't share his faith. After three hours of keyed-up expectancy, he was beginning to feel a little cheated.

With a sigh the rocket pilot swung into his fifteenth circuit, wondering just how long this would have to go on.

And then it came. They all saw it in the same instant— an arrowhead of light curving smoothly out of the void. Visible at more than a hundred thousand feet, it took almost two minutes to drop down to the inspection rocket's altitude. The starship passed it at a distance of five or six miles, in a slow arc extending toward the northern segment of Copernicus.

"Godalmighty, it's going to touch down!" shouted the Co-ordinator. "Follow it," he snapped to the pilot, "and drop as close as you can."

Even as the rocket changed course the now hovering starship achieved a perfect touch-down stance.

At the same time the professor had become deathly pale, his eyes displaying a sudden vacancy. Then he spoke. The voice was familiar to Jansen.

Not, however, as the voice of Otto Reigner.

"Man's future lies far out in space, but his past belongs to the terrestrial jungle. Some day he will learn to reach for the stars without avarice. But only when he sees no jungle in the sky. That is why this first voyage must end in . . ."

The voice fell to a whisper and was silent.

Simultaneously there was a flash of brilliant light.

Jansen turned sharply to the observation frame and gazed out across the crater. At one thousand feet the starship hung suspended. Then it appeared to unfold in great petals of flame. And for a moment the crater was drenched with light. Then the white-hot debris dropped slowly through the lunar silence.

When there was nothing more to be seen the Co-ordinator turned to Reigner angrily. "Well, I hope you're satisfied with—" He stopped. He was speaking to a dead man.

Or, as he told himself grimly, two dead men.

He looked at the shrunken figure, at the gray, weary face, and thought of all that Otto Reigner had endured in the three days it had taken him to die.

Eventually the pilot said, "Still want me to go down?"

"No, it doesn't matter now."

The pilot, a youngster of twenty-one, was filled with curiosity. He put the rocket into a slow climb and switched over to automatic. Then he went to have a look at the body.

"Co-ordinator, what did he mean—that bit about a jungle in the sky?"

Co-ordinator Jansen gave a harsh laugh. "You don't know? Then I'll tell you, son. He meant that we're all just a bunch of clever apes; that civilization's only skin-deep; and that we're not fit to go shoving our hairy fingers into deep space."

The pilot thought it over. Then he said, "Personally, I'd rather be a clever ape than a crazy human."

Jansen gazed through the observation frame at the hard, receding peaks of Copernicus. He gave another bitter laugh.

"Got any idea which is which?"

41

THE BUTTERFLIES

The survey ship *Prometheus* dropped into orbit four hundred miles above the surface of Planet Five. Altogether there were seven planets in the system. They belonged to the Companion of Sirius, a "white dwarf," which had the distinction of being the first star to be recognized by terrestrial astronomers before it could be seen.

Planet Five was twenty-two million miles from the mother sun. Sirius itself lay far beyond the confines of the tiny system, being another eighteen hundred million miles away. To the crew of the *Prometheus* it presented a bright blinding disc, no less impressive than that of its now relatively near Companion. Eventually the *Prometheus* would voyage closer to the great star to survey her single red planet. But meanwhile the Companion's system seemed infinitely more attractive—an explorer's paradise.

When the orbit maneuver had been successfully completed the crew of four took themselves to the mess-deck for a celebration. They had something to celebrate, for, so far as they knew, the Prometheus was the first ship to navigate satisfactorily under what was called the relativity drive—in memory of a very great man and a very imperfect theory.

As soon as they took their places at table the electronic cooker disgorged roast chicken and a wealth of elegant trimmings, and the refrigerator surrendered a magnum of champagne. Only three of the crew, however, were able to savor the luxury of drinking wine eight and a half light-years away from the vineyard that produced it; for the fourth, a positronic robot, preferred to dine infrequently on a large helping of amperes.

Presently Captain Trenoy, physicist, astronomer and master of the *Prometheus,* gave a formal toast; while Whizbang, the robot, watched with red expressionless eyes.

"May our explorations be fruitful," said Captain Trenoy, raising his glass, "may our return be safe and may the time drag not be too heavy on us."

"Amen," said Dr. Blane

He and Dr. Luiss regarded each other gravely as they lifted their glasses in response. They were both thinking about the same thing. The journey of eight and a half light-years had taken the *Prometheus* eighteen *kinetic* months, but the ship had left the Solar System fifteen Earth-years before.

By the time it returned, more than thirty-five Earth-years would have gone by, though the crew would have aged a mere three and a half years.

Blane, who combined the duties of psychologist, surgeon and physician, was contemplating the spiritual effect of being cut off from one's time and generation. Fortunately or otherwise, it was a problem that would have no reality until the *Prometheus* touched down on Earth once more.

Luiss, who held the departments of biochemistry and geology, stared at his champagne and wondered just how long it would take him to go mad.

But such disturbing thoughts slid rapidly into the background as Captain Trenoy, refilling the three glasses, turned the conversation to the immediate problem of touching down on Planet Five. After eighteen months of monotonous starflight, during which there was little to do but make routine checks, routine researches, routine conversation, it was pleasant if unnerving to be faced with the necessity for action.

"Here endeth the first lesson," said the captain, with obscure irony. "And now we'd better fix up some orderly procedure. I am assuming, of course, that you feel we ought to explore as soon as possible." He gazed at his companions inquiringly.

"No reason why we shouldn't," said Dr. Luiss. "I've checked Whizbang's preliminary findings. It doesn't seem there will be much difficulty."

"I haven't any objections," agreed Blane. Then he added with a dry smile: "But in view of our experience of the unusual effects of star-sickness, it might be advisable if we sent Whizbang by himself on the first trip."

"I was about to suggest that myself," said Trenoy. "It would be an elementary safety procedure. I think, too, that we should fix it so that we can control the landing rocket from here, just in case Whizbang comes to grief. It would be disastrous if we lost a ferry rocket on the first landing."

"What makes you think I might come to grief, Captain?" boomed the robot. "The findings indicate that it's going to be a smooth job."

Trenoy laughed. "You're as logical as they come, Whizbang," he said. "But we poor mortals, lacking your mental equipment, tend to be just a little superstitious. To us, as to the primeval savages, the unknown is always a little magical—in spite of science, in spite of reason and in spite of infallible robots."

Whizbang made strange noises, which his companions had

long since learned to interpret as robotic laughter.

"So I noticed," he retorted, "when we changed down to planetary drive out of R.D. Dr. Blane, our eminent psychologist, was, I recall, furiously stroking a rabbit's paw."

Blane smiled. "No need to feel superior, Whizbang. I saw you playing with a new set of logarithmic notations. It was the first time I've ever seen a robot doodling."

"All right, doodler," said Captain Trenoy. "Tell us what you've discovered about Planet Five, and we'll decide if there is likely to be difficulty."

Whizbang recited his information with monotonous efficiency. "Size equates approximately with terrestrial moon. Mass: one over eighty-three point two. Density: three point seven nine. Orbital period: ninety-eight days. Surface: three-fifths solid. Atmosphere: oxygen helium, forty-five fifty. Vegetation: low type scrub with unusual predominance of blue. No evidence yet of animal life."

"Suppose we put you down," said Luiss. "What would you do?"

"Take out *Radiac* and test at ground level," answered Whizbang promptly. "Collect samples and explore to a radius of one hundred yards. Radio verbal report to Captain Trenoy and await instructions."

"Fair enough," said Trenoy. "Down you go."

"I've already checked the ferry rocket," announced Whizbang. "*Radiac* and sample jars are aboard." He stood up and stretched his nine feet of steel and duralumin. "Shall I make ready, sir?" he asked formally.

"No time like the present," said Trenoy. "Go ahead. Come back and tell us five minutes before point of exit."

The three men stood on the navigation deck of the *Prometheus,* watching the small ferry rocket drift out of the orbit. As it receded in slow motion Whizbang waved a metal arm cheerily to them from inside his plastiglass dome.

"Are we going to stabilize position over his landing area?" asked Dr. Blane.

"Might as well," said the captain. "There's no reason for playing safe on fuel. Thank God those days are over."

The ferry rocket, gathering negative speed, dropped like a silver bullet to the vast brown and crimson stretch of lava plains below.

"The atmosphere is a piece of cake," said Dr. Luiss happily. "It looks as though we shall be able to throw off our pressure suits and jump about freely at one-sixth gravity."

44

"It may be my natural pessimism," observed Dr. Blane, "but I have an odd notion that Planet Five is altogether too obliging. Something tells me that we are in for a few surprises."

"I think you're right," agreed Trenoy. "There always are surprises in this kind of work. It would be somewhat surprising if there weren't." He turned his attention to the two-way radio. "*Prometheus* to Whizbang. *Prometheus* to Whizbang. How are you doing? Over."

He turned a switch, and Whizbang's voice came loud and clear. "Whizbang to Captain Trenoy. I'm skating cautiously through the boundaries of the stratosphere at a hundred thousand feet. Velocity five thousand. Fin temperature fifteen hundred. Internal temperature one hundred and three. It's easy going. Over."

"What does the surface look like?" asked Trenoy.

"As expected, Captain. Blue vegetation areas change shade slightly, purple to crimson. But this may be due to invisible cloud. Over."

"Are you using the auto-pilot? Over." asked the captain. He heard the robot laugh.

"I am more efficient, sir. The auto-pilot would take three minutes longer. Over."

"Watch that fin temperature!" snapped Trenoy. "It's more important than trying to beat the auto-pilot. Over and out."

"Yes, sir. Over and out." Whizbang did his best to sound metallically aggrieved.

Seven minutes later he touched the ferry rocket down to a perfect landing.

"Whizbang to *Prometheus*. I have touched down on the agreed area on Planet Five. Landing normal. Fuel consumption subnormal. What are your orders? Over."

Back on the *Prometheus*, Captain Trenoy gripped the mike, glancing at the two men with controlled excitement. He flicked the switch and spoke to Whizbang.

"Do not move. Describe the landscape. Over."

"Sunlight strength four," said Whizbang. "Sky purple to deep blue. Horizon bounded by mountain range. Estimated height of highest peak nine thousand feet. Distance twelve miles. Planetary surface: rock, crimson, brown, black. Nearest vegetation three hundred yards away. Pampas type grass, four to six foot high. Color blue to crimson. Occasional bushes with tendril type leaves, rising to ten feet. Color yellow to gold. Animal life: butterfly type, wing-span nine to fifteen inches, multicolored, present in large numbers. Estimated cloud of twenty to thirty circling ferry rocket. Large clouds in constant motion above pampas. Over."

On the navigation deck of the survey ship the atmosphere of excitement intensified.

"Butterflies!" exclaimed Dr. Luiss. "This is going to be interesting. They're quite a reasonably developed evolutionary structure. Obviously there will be other examples of animal life, even if they're only vestigial species relating to the butterflies' development."

Dr. Blane laughed. "Maybe we'll have to take nets with us and dash around like three bug-collecting schoolboys. At one-sixth G we ought to be able to chase 'em on the wing."

"Not so fast," said Trenoy. "Let's see how they react to Whizbang and he to them." He flicked the radio switch and spoke once more to the robot, who sat patiently in the pilot's seat of the ferry rocket four hundred miles below.

"*Prometheus* to Whizbang. Take out your *Radiac*, your atmospherometer and the cine-camera. Make five tests for radioactivity—one general and four specific. Find out the pressure and bulk gases and bring samples back for lab work. Then take your camera and use fifteen minutes of film. Spread it out—panoramic stuff, telephoto, microphoto and general interest. Also get a butterfly if possible—without harming it. Over."

"Yes, sir,' 'answered Whizbang. "When shall I report? Over."

"Don't be lazy," said Trenoy. "Clip the transceiver on your chest. We'll want a record while you're operating. Over."

"As you say, Captain. Would you like a commentary or question and answer? Over."

"Commentary will do. If I want to ask questions I'll break in. Over and out."

The men on the navigation deck waited for the robot's monologue to begin. Dr. Luiss went to the manual telescope and began to search the landing area with it. After a moment or two, fancying a shiny dot that he'd picked out was the ferry rocket, he called Captain Trenoy to take a look. Then Whizbang launched into his commentary.

"Transceiver clipped on. I am now descending through oubliette with *Radiac*. Pressure equalized at nine point nine. Ladder down and entry-port released. I am going down the ladder. General radioactivity normal for oxygen helium at nine point nine. Will now proceed fifty yards from rocket for four radial tests."

Trenoy switched across. "How are the butterflies reacting to your presence?"

"They don't appear to have noticed me yet. . . . Am now making first of radial tests. . . . The butterflies have just begun to notice me. The ones circling above the rocket aren't being tempted, but another cloud of about fifty has risen from the pampas. They're heading straight for me. Now they're circling overhead."

"See if you can get one, but don't harm them if it can be helped," said Trenoy.

"They're fast on the wing, Captain, and they seem to be able to estimate my range. They're concentrating about twenty feet above my headpiece."

There was a long pause, then: "Flutter by, butterfly! Flutter, flutter, butterfly. Well, well, well! Cut off my co-ordinators and call me a computer. I think that I shall never see a robot beautiful as me." For the first time in his existence Whizbang sounded as though he was trying to sing. It was an unmelodious robotic howl. To the men on the *Prometheus* it sounded midway between ecstasy and insanity.

With a startled oath Captain Trenoy switched in. "Whizbang! What the devil's happening?"

There was no answer for several seconds, then a slurred voice mumbled, "Steel, steel, glorious steel! You'll never know how metallic I feel."

"Whizbang! Answer my question!" Trenoy put every ounce of authority into his command. The response was not encouraging:

"With nuts on his fingers and bolts on his toes, Whizbang needs oiling wherever he goes." The voice trailed away to a crooning whisper. Then silence.

The three men stared at each other in consternation.

"He's off his head," snapped Luiss. "Some damn silly short-circuilt has given him D.T.'s."

Dr. Blane looked thoughtful. "He was perfectly all right until those butterflies began to concentrate. I wonder . . ."

"What are you thinking of—radiation?" asked Captain Trenoy.

"Something like that," agreed Blane. "It doesn't sound like a mechanical breakdown. I've never heard of a robot getting light headed because of a short-circuit. It's as if something—some force—had disturbed his equilibrium."

"The ST-EX robots were proofed against every known type of radiation before we left Earth," objected the captain.

"I know," said Blane. "But obviously this is something they

weren't proofed against."

"The simple solution is usually correct," said Luiss. "He's had a breakdown in the language areas. He was all right while he was in the rocket."

"I'll try him again," said Trenoy. He switched over. "Whizbang! Can you hear me? Over."

Silence.

"Whizbang! What's happening? Over."

Silence.

"Whizbang! I order you back to the rocket Make ready to return to ship! Over."

Still silence.

"Where do we go from here?" asked Captain Trenoy at length. "Any suggestions, gentlemen?"

"Somebody will have to go down in the reserve rocket," said Dr. Luiss. "That somebody had better be me."

"Control your curiosity and be rational," reproved Dr. Blane. "What's the point of hazarding our only other rocket *and* a human being? Have another think."

"Total control!" exclaimed the captain. "The servo-mechanisms for the oubliette and entry-port were synchonized with the auto-pilot before Whizbang went down. Even if we can't get him back to the ferry rocket we can bring the rocket back here. Then someone might go down and see what's happened to him."

Before Captain Trenoy settled down at the remote control panel he made a further effort to contact the enigmatic robot but met with no success. While he was bringing the rocket back to the four-hundred-mile orbit Blane and Luiss developed a quiet and friendly argument concerning the probable cause of Whizbang's failure to respond. Then, since Whizbang still presumably had the transceiver on his chest, Dr. Blane tried to break down his problematic silence by a series of commands, exhortations, trick statements and desperate pleas for help. He met with no result.

"You see," said Luiss triumphantly. "It's a mechanical breakdown. If he won't even let out a bleat when you tell him it's a matter of life and death, it means only one thing: somewhere the circuit is wrecked."

Dr. Blane still shook his head. "Robots have certain powers of volition," he said slowly. "Weaker, of course, than human volition. Now let us suppose, for the purpose of hypothesis, that something with greater than human volition was able to establish contact with him. Suppose it *willed* him to disobey orders."

48

'Moonshine," pronounced Dr. Luiss skeptically. "Are you suggesting that Whizbang got himself hypnotized? Because if so, you're getting unnecessarily melodramatic."

"One has to consider possibilities," said Dr. Blane evenly.

"But that's an impossibility! You might just as well consider the possibility of the ground opening up and swallowing him."

"It can't be ruled out," said Blane without humor. "Who are we to assume that the life forms on Planet Five behave conventionally? Those butterflies, for example, might—"

"Might lay duck eggs," grinned Luiss. "Go take a sedative, Doctor. Your imagination is slightly fantastic."

"So, very often, is the truth," retorted Blane.

While he had been talking Dr. Blane had watched the progress of the ferry rocket by radar screen and visulator. He saw now that it was within ordinary visual range and, not wishing to prolong a useless discussion, climbed into the astrodome to watch it "dock" alongside the *Prometheus*.

"I still think one man only should go and that he should not leave the rocket—unless, of course, he finds a reasonable explanation for Whizbang's silence." Watching the captain closely Dr. Blane could see, even before he replied, that Trenoy was unconvinced.

"Perhaps you are letting superstition take precedence over scientific caution," said Captain Trenoy, with the faintest of smiles. "I think our arrangements will be quite adequate. We shall take u/s vibrators and H.F.C. beam apparatus. Unless there is an emergency one of us will remain in the rocket all the time."

"You may encounter something against which the vibrators and H.F.C. weapon will be useless."

"In that case it certainly won't be physical," observed Dr. Luiss with irony.

"Exactly," said Blane. He wanted to add something else but couldn't find the right words.

"We'd better get moving," remarked Trenoy. "We may have a small search on our hands before we find Whizbang."

Dr. Blane accepted defeat gracefully. "Good hunting," he said. "I'll be glued to the transceiver."

"We'll bring you back a couple of tame butterflies to play with," promised Luiss gaily, as he fixed the headpiece on his pressure suit.

When they had checked their pressure and their personal

radios the two men left the navigation deck and made their way to the starboard airlock and entry-port. From the astrodome Dr. Blane watched the small ferry rocket fall out of the obit as it gathered negative speed. Twenty minutes later he heard Luiss's voice telling him that they had touched down safely at the landing area.

"We can see Whizbang," said Luis excitedly. "He's about a couple of hundred yards away, balancing on one foot like a heavyweight ballerina. The butterflies are still circling over him." He chuckled. "Bet they're thinking that if he's a speciemn of alien culture they did well to remain butterflies. He looks, though, almost as if he belonged to the landscape."

"Any other signs of life—apart from the butterflies?" asked Dr. Blane.

"No, not yet. I'm going out to have a look at our petrified robot, so I'll hand over to Captain Trenoy."

Dr. Blane's hands were trembling, his face was white. He paced the navigation deck rapidly, casting suspicious glances now and again at the nine-foot robot, who stood waiting patiently.

"Tell me your story again," he commanded. "We will consider the inaccuracy in relation to the whole." It was no good calling the robot a liar, because Whizbang was mechanically incapable of lying. He was, however, quite capable of being inaccurate.

Responding to the order, he again related his story in a voice which faltered only very slightly when he came to the part which Dr. Blane was able to disprove.

"The first thing I remember, sir," said Whizbang, "was Dr. Luiss bawling at me for being what he called a brokendown cretin. Previous to that my only recollection is of reporting back to ship as I began the first radial test and the butterflies came."

"Where were the butterflies when Dr. Luiss spoke to you?"

"They were circling the rocket again, sir, but there were none near me or Dr. Luiss. The clouds skimming over the pampas seemed bigger than before, but that was probably because Dr. Luiss had disturbed them. He told me he'd given the group circling above my head half a second of ultrasonic vibration and that it had scared them away."

"Did he tell you his further intentions?"

"He said he was going to look around within a hundred-yard radius and collect samples. Then he ordered me back to the rocket."

"What did Captain Trenoy do?"

"He questioned me and then spoke to you, sir, describing the landscape in detail and giving you a commentary on Dr. Luiss's activities."

"Why did Captain Trenoy leave the rocket?"

"Dr. Luiss called to him over the personal wave length in a very excited voice. He said that he'd found the skeleton of a large quadruped with a cranial capacity of approximately one cubic foot. He said that the animals on Planet Five must have reached a very high evolutionary stage. Finally he suggested that Captain Trenoy come and have a look for himself, leaving me in the rocket. The captain said it didn't seem a very intelligent procedure, but Dr. Luiss replied that there were no living animals in sight, that the pampas was far enough away to give a reasonable safety margin and that if the butterflies came near they could certainly be dispersed by ultrasonics."

Dr. Blane nodded. "That's true. I heard snatches of their conversation over the transceiver. Did Captain Trenoy give you any instructions before he left?"

"He put me through a simple test to make sure that my memory and reasoning ability were not damaged. Then he told me to stay in the rocket and not leave it under any circumstances."

"At which point," said Dr. Blane thoughtfully, "you took over the commentary."

"That is so," agreed Whizbang, with a trace of hesitation. "I continued with the commentary until you gave me instructions to return to the *Prometheus*."

"But since I did not radio those instructions," said Blane, staring hard at the robot, "we are left with two possibilities. Name them!"

The robot was silent for a moment. Then he spoke slowly. "One: that my circuits are damaged. Two: that some other entity caused me to receive the message."

"Which do you think it is?" snapped Blane.

"If you would like to test me, sir . . ." began Whizbang.

"To hell with tests! Which is it?"

"I think my circuits are intact."

"Then you think the message originated elsewhere?"

"Yes, sir—if you are sure you did not send it."

Blane controlled himself with difficulty. "We'll leave that for the moment. Repeat verbatim your commentary to the point where I apparently ordered you to return."

"Whizbang to *Prometheus*," said the robot. "Captain Trenoy

is now descending through the oubliette to join Dr. Luiss. Dr. Luiss is examining the skeleton of the quadruped. The nearest butterflies are about two hundred yards away. There is a small cloud of them rising from the pampas. They appear to be circling aimlessly at an altitude of a hundred and fifty feet. Captain Trenoy has now joined Dr. Luiss. They are digging together by the side of the skeleton. The butterflies are drifting slightly. Captain Trenoy glances at them every few seconds, while continuing his work. Now the cloud is almost above the skeleton at about two hundred feet. Suddenly the two men stand up. They stare at the butterflies. Dr. Luiss remarks over his personal radio that it is the most incredible thing he ever heard. Suddenly the butterflies drop fifty feet. At the same time Captain Trenoy and Dr. Luiss begin to unscrew their headpieces very slowly. . . ." Whizbang stopped.

"Go on! Go on!" urged Dr. Blane.

"Then, sir," said Whizbang, "I heard your voice through the transceiver. You said: '*Prometheus* to Whizbang. Return to orbit immediately. Urgent! Return to orbit immediately. Over and out.' "

"What happened next?" asked Blane.

"I informed Captain Trenoy over the ground radio. He said, 'You must obey, Whizbang. You must always obey.' So I sealed the rocket and took off as rapidly as possible. By the time I had equalized gravity and was beginning to release power the butterflies had dropped another fifty feet. Captain Trenoy and Dr. Luiss were standing motionless. They had taken off their headpieces. Then I had to let in power and the rocket climbed."

"Was Captain Trenoy's voice normal?"

"No, sir. He spoke slowly and very quietly."

"Are you sure it was his voice?"

"Yes, sir."

For two or three minutes Dr. Blane strode nervously up and down, tortured by indecision. Finally he made up his mind.

"I am going down, Whizbang."

"Yes, sir."

"You will remain on duty here."

Dr. Blane set the rocket down gently. He unstrapped himself, stood up and gazed through the plastiglass dome. A quarter of a mile away he saw two motionless figures standing erect on a stretch of brown and crimson rock. Focusing the binoculars, Dr. Blane made out a cloud of butterfliflies hovering about ten feet above the men. The heads of his two companions were strangely obscured, but dull sunlight glinted on the surface of a headpiece lying at the feet of one of them.

Grimly Dr. Blane reached for the two u/s vibrators. Placing them carefully in the pockets of his pressure suit, he descended through the oubliette. A few seconds later he stood on the strange surface of Planet Five.

Gripping a vibrator in each hand he looked cautiously around him and then up at the sky. Apart from the cloud above the two men a quarter of a mile away and the endless activity on the pampas there did not seem to be any immediate danger.

Slowly Dr. Blane walked toward his companions. At one hundred yards he stopped, stood quite still, took careful aim. He gave the cloud of butterflies a two second dose of vibration. They scattered with much violent flapping and a few dropped crazily down to the rocky surface. As they fell, another small cloud rose and Dr. Blane knew then what had been obscuring the heads of Trenoy and Luiss. He fought back a sharp involuntary sickness and marched on.

At fifty yards he thought it was an illusion, but at twenty-five yards it became inescapable fact. Dr. Blane was approaching two men in pressure suits who were dead but still standing. Their clean-picked skulls were fixed in two barren grins.

In his own pressure suit Blane was sweating with panic. A sixth sense warned him to turn around and run. But it was already too late. For to Dr. Blane's heightened perception there came the first faint strains of a vast, compelling music. It was the pattern, the experience, the mobility, the sheer harmony of a thousand symphonies condensed into a single chord.

Turning, with a tremendous effort, he saw the butterflies rising from the pampas and knew—in the instant before that colossal theme of ecstasy blocked all thought—that presently the butterflies would begin to circle lower and lower.

There were tears in Dr. Blane's eyes. But they were not tears for his own approaching death. They were the only way in which he, and his companions before him, could react to an experience that was profound beyond any known to man; that was compelling and final, tearing its way past the flimsy threshold of human consciousness.

The vibrators dropped from his impatient fingers. Slowly, hypnotically, Dr. Blane fumbled for the release clips of his headpiece. And the music swelled like sacramental thunder, the soundless music of thousands of multicolored butterflies, thousands of insect carnivores closing in upon their selected

53

prey. And across the pampas, across the brown and crimson rocks, myriads of flapping wings proclaimed their centralization of power—submergence of the individual in a tremendous group identity.

Dr. Blane stood there unable to think, unable to see, unable to move—waiting for the butterflies to descend. Waiting for the crunch of small but powerful mandibles. . . .

The short nine-hour day on Planet Five drew quietly to a close. Then the sun, known to earthlings as the Companion of Sirius, began to slip smoothly over a blue and purple horizon. Presently the butterflies rose, winging across the pampas to their nocturnal batlike roosts. Presently there was only the solitude of night, the remote mystery of stars. . . .

The survey ship *Prometheus* remained in orbit for ten more days. Whizbang kept a steady vigil by the transceiver on the navigation deck, in accordance with instruction. But the lack of response to his repeated signals forced him to the obvious conclusion.

He satisfied himself that there was one very sound reason why there could be no survivors: for men, unlike robots, cannot exist without water. Unfortunately, the water on Planet Five was different from its terrestrial counterpart.

So Whizbang brought in an open verdict, secure in the conviction that his masters could no longer be alive.

He had, however, no knowledge of the manner of their deaths. When he, too, had been a victim of the butterfly-mind, he had not heard the compelling music, for it was reaching to something far deeper than a synthetic brain. He had merely been positronically disturbed. He had merely been, for the first time in his robotic existence, asleep while his batteries were still powered. Nor could he know that, with a superior act of volition, the butterfly-mind had simply willed him to go away. Being metallic, he was not a possible source of food; and not being a source of food, he was only irrelevant.

But even a robot must rationalize when forced to act without human command. So Whizbang had found it necessary to "invent" Dr. Blane's instruction to return to the *Prometheus*.

Standing now on the navigation deck he stared with red expressionless eyes at the surface of Planet Five.

At last he reached a decision. The information would have to be given to other human beings, who would then assume responsibility.

Whizbang jerked himself up into the astrodome and began to take bearings. As he worked, he knew neither happiness nor anxiety, neither hope nor despair, neither regret nor relief.

He knew only that he could handle the relativity drive more efficiently than men.

REPEAT PERFORMANCE

Sheridan woke up suddenly with a faint high-pitched humming in his ears—like the sound of a remote machine. Immediately he knew there was a dream he should try to remember, a dream that had some terrible bearing on reality.

He lay there for a few moments, gazing dully at the ceiling, while the humming died away. Then he tried to think, tried to imagine the sort of dream that would make his forehead damp with sweat and his limbs tremble. But he received no enlightenment. Whatever it was, the dream had now faded away completely down long misty canyons of darkness.

Presently the tension began to drain out of him, giving way to a reasonably calm sense of expectancy. He got out of bed, stretched, and began to dress. As he moved around the room, he noticed—curiously—that all the furniture and fittings were still in exactly the same places. It was an odd thing to notice. . . . Odder still, that he should wish for some slight change.

Indulging a sudden fancy, he picked up the small bedside table and placed it by the window. Then, feeling as if he'd achieved something, he finished dressing.

But as he sat on the edge of the bed and bent down to lace his shoes the humming came again—briefly, more distant. He paused, haunted by a vague recollection, and knew beyond any shadow of doubt that the telephone was going to ring.

Seconds passed; then from downstairs in the hall came a burst of echoing sound. The rhythmic summons of the telephone, demanding a response, hammered vigorously at his sense of unreality. Hurrying along the landing, Sheridan found it easy to dismiss clairvoyance with a shrug.

After all, what was so wonderful about anticipating a phone call by five seconds? His life revolved around phone calls. As a doctor he would be subconsciously expecting them all the time.

He sat on the edge of the hall table and reached for the receiver. Then his hand stopped in mid-air, hesitated for a moment and dropped toward his pocket, fumbling for cigarettes and matches. The phone continued to ring.

Lighting a cigarette, he saw that his hands were shaking. He knew why. He knew whose voice he was going to hear.

There was a vital moment of decision, when he felt free to make the choice. Or was it just a hoax? Was he only doing what he *had* to do? Gripping the receiver, he realized that he would never know. Sheridan took a deep breath and lifted destiny off the hook.

"I want to speak to Dr. Sheridan, please." Her voice was a shade high. Usually it was low and vibrant.

"Speaking," said Sheridan. "Hello, Ann. Long time no see. How are you?"

"Richard!" She sounded relieved. "Thank heaven it's you. I was afraid I was going to get the Bedside Manner. . . . He would have been useless."

"The senior partner wouldn't like that," said Sheridan dryly. "Incidentally, is this call personal, or professional?"

"Both. Richard, are you very busy?"

"Not this time of the year. Everybody is too darn healthy. I'm lucky if I get half a dozen consultations a day—barring accidents."

"Good. I'm the accident. I want you to come over to Redgrave as soon as possible. It's fairly urgent."

Sheridan tried hard to ignore the vivid picture associated with this voice, but he couldn't. He saw Ann Blackmore just as clearly as if she were with him. He saw the tall, stately figure; the pale, slightly irregular features framed by an abundance of dark hair; the faraway eyes, and that odd, one-sided smile. There were more beautiful women; but this one happened to be the girl he had loved. He wondered, hopelessly, if he would have to go through it all again.

Go through it all again! A dangerous thought. He threw it aside quickly and concentrated on what he was saying.

"I think I can make it by about eleven-thirty. . . . Why the panic?"

"It's Daddy. I think he's going mad."

Nice timing, thought Sheridan grimly, and a restrained delivery, too. Ann was still the fine actress, never throwing a good line away, always giving it just the right emphasis.

He said, "Or maybe he's just going sane. Anyone who has a Nobel prize for physics is entitled to go sane once in a while. Now tell me what it's all about—clinically."

Ann gave a smooth interpretation of a high-spirited girl losing her temper. "For God's sake, Richard! Stop being the

56

cynical lover! You don't think I called you just to play games, do you? I need someone badly; I need help. If there had been another good doctor within ten miles I'd certainly have—"

"Naturally," cut in Sheridan. "But I'm still waiting for the facts."

There was a pause, a sigh. Anger or frustration? He wondered.

"All right—Doctor," said Ann. "Facts, nothing but facts: I came to Redgrave on Friday. I hadn't seen him for two or three months, so I thought I'd snatch a few days before rehearsals. . . . I didn't realize he'd become so—so withdrawn. But he goes around talking to himself, Richard. He doesn't seem to know whether it's day or night, winter or summer."

"Concentration," suggested Sheridan. "A lot of the top scientists are like that. They spend so much time concentrating they just can't stop. It becomes obsessional."

"But he forgets to eat. He'll just sit there staring at the table, murmuring about his damned machine. I'm frightened."

"What machine?"

"It's good for a laugh, anyway," said Ann bitterly. "He's working on a time machine; at least, that's what he says. . . . Now tell me he's still with us!"

Sheridan was silent for a moment, considering the labyrinthine genius of Professor Robert Blackmore; a man whose work in wave mechanics was revolutionary, and whose name ranked with those of Bohr, Heisenberg, Schroedinger—even Einstein.

It was more than a year since he had seen Professor Blackmore, but Sheridan retained a sharp mental picture of the man: white-haired, vigorous, with an ability to soar over cautious theories to results that only he realized were attainable. No indication at all of waning powers. On the contrary, it had seemed that Blackmore's best years lay ahead.

But that was a year ago. A lot could happen in a year.

"Well, say something," pleaded Ann. "Tell me he's crazy or senile. Tell me he's harmless. . . . It couldn't be a serious project, could it?"

"I just don't know," confessed Sheridan. "Since they cracked the atom, conventional scientific theory has been having a lost weekend. Nobody's sure about anything any more. It could be that your father is merely battering his overworked brains out on a large blank wall. But I suppose there's still the chance that he's on the track of something. I'll have a better idea when I've seen him."

"Sorry to drag you in, Richard, after what's happened."

57

She even sounded as though she meant it.

"That's all right. You're quite sure it's a time machine?"

"I ought to be. I've had the wretched thing mumbled at me incessantly. Get here soon, won't you? My nerves are pretty well shot to pieces. Besides, he has an experiment planned for midday and it would be more than our lives are worth to drag him out of the lab."

"I'll make it as fast as I can," he promised. "By the sound of it, you're the one who needs treatment. Would you like a sedative?"

"Not the kind you're offering."

A thin smile played on Sheridan's lips. "Is that meant to be enigmatic?"

Ann had recovered herself sufficiently to give a slightly artificial laugh. "I don't know. Think about it. Good-bye, Richard, and thank you."

"Good-by, Ann." He heard the line go dead, and slowly put the receiver down.

Suddenly, he was aware of that faint humming again, as if the universe had turned into a vast electric clock and he was sitting right on top of the mechanism.

He looked around him, experiencing a vague shimmer of unreality. Somehow the house had become a cardboard house, a piece of stage scenery, with himself and Ann running through the lines of an unwritten script. . . .

Of course it was nothing—nothing but damned imagination. A seedy half-hour for a man who'd just had the starch scared out of him by a nightmare he couldn't remember. It was the sort of feeling that would be blasted out of existence by a good solid breakfast. The sort of panic that would drown in the first cup of coffee.

As if in response to a signal, he heard domestic noises coming from the kitchen. The sizzling, the clatter of pans. the smell of cooking. All very normal. Then Mrs. Fagan, the old Irish housekeeper poking her head round the door with: "Come along, now, Dr. Sheridan. Sure, you'll be needing something warm inside of you. It's a frosty morning."

Sheridan registered the fact that it was indeed a cool morning. He shivered, and went in to breakfast, trying not to notice that he was sweating.

Normality was short-lived. It lasted—without a great deal of conviction—through breakfast. But Sheridan had no appetite, and even while he was toying with the food on his plate he felt the need to tell himself that all was well with

58

the world while ham and eggs still continued to look like ham and eggs.

Presently he got tired of trying to convince himself that he was hungry, and decided that the best antidote for the peculiar feeling of tension would be a brisk session of work. He went into the consulting room, glanced at the few names on his desk pad, and knew that he was waiting for something. He knew what it was; knew, also, that it would begin in ten or fifteen seconds.

He looked at his watch; saw the thin red finger jerk slowly round. On the thirteenth second the faint humming recurred. It seemed a shade louder this time, pulsating in his skull; an obscure, rhythmic threat.

He did something he'd never done before, in ten years of general practice. He opened the bottom drawer of his desk and took out a bottle of brandy, then poured himself a stiff dose of Dutch courage. It took care of the humming for a while and enabled him to face the few waiting patients.

He wanted to ask them whether they too had heard it; if they, too, felt that the morning was somehow twisted all out of shape. But something stopped him—the look in their eyes, maybe. Mechanically he went through the routine examinations, the routine questions. There was only one question he was afraid to ask.

Eventually he dealt with the last patient, closed the consulting room door and slumped loosely in his chair. He lit a cigarette, inhaled deeply and allowed himself to consider his approaching visit to Redgrave and Ann.

He remembered his last trip to that old Victorian country house: the time he came home with a returned engagement ring in his pocket. A few centuries ago—at least, that was how it felt.

Would Ann still have the same power over him? Would she be able to twist him around her little finger? He began to regret his promise, began to dread the appointment for two separate reasons.

The second reason was Robert Blackmore. Sheridan realized that the situation must be pretty rough to make Ann swallow her pride and turn to him for help. Though her emotions were volatile, though she was characteristically impetuous—as Sheridan knew to his cost—she was not one to lose her nerve easily. She would not have called him unless there was something really wrong, something that wouldn't wait.

He tried to reconcile Ann's account of her father's present

59

condition with his own impression of Robert Blackmore at their last meeting, over a year ago. It was impossible to believe that he had retired so completely into a dream world. A year ago Blackmore had combined the ambition of a man half his age with the imaginative drive of a child prodigy. And yet, according to Ann, he had now regressed into a kind of fantasy state.

But suppose the rest of the world was crazy and Professor Blackmore was sane! Suppose a time machine was theoretically possible. For a while Sheridan sat there, fascinated by the thought.

Suddenly he glanced at his watch. Eleven thirty-five. He had told Ann he would be at Redgrave by eleven thirty. With a smothered exclamation he jumped to his feet, remembering her warning about the experiment at midday.

As he hurried out to his car, the sharp morning air swept over him like a subtle stimulant, easing his taut nerves and restoring vitality to his body. Soon he was driving quickly out of town, heading for a short cut, a narrow lane that snaked along for about five miles until it came to the old country house.

Glancing once more at the time, he saw that it was already ten minutes to twelve. He put his foot down on the accelerator.

At two minutes past twelve, he reached a short avenue, bordered by elm trees, that was the main entrance to Redgrave.

Ann was waiting for him, standing by the massive paneled door, looking as though she had been there quite a time. Even as he approached, Sheridan could see the tension in her expression ease a little with relief. He switched the engine off, got out of the car and managed to greet her with a smile.

With a certain detachment, he noticed that unhappiness added to her beauty.

"You've been such a long time, Richard." There was a controlled reproach in her voice.

"I was delayed," he said, and that was true enough—delayed chiefly by cowardice. "Where's the Old Man—busy knocking the mainspring out of time?" He tried to sound nonchalant.

She nodded. "He's in the lab." And her glance strayed up to a high window belonging to the large attic that Robert Blackmore had converted for his own purposes.

"Would you like me to go straight up?"

"Please, not just yet. I want you to myself for a minute or two. Richard, I need you badly—you don't know how much. Maybe I'm going mad, too. I keep hearing a strange humming that seems to reverberate through the house—distant, but always near. Sometimes, almost inside me. It's as if . . ." She paused uncertainly. "You'd better come inside. You can't cope with a hysterical woman on the doorstep."

As soon as she mentioned the humming Sheridan felt a curious coldness pass through his limbs. Automatically he followed her into the house.

She was just about to open a door leading off the hall when Sheridan placed his hand gently on her shoulder. She turned around to face him with a mute pleading. Sheridan took her hand—colder even than his own.

"Ann, I've heard it, too. It seemed to be connected with a dream I had—one that I couldn't remember."

She turned deathly pale and swayed slightly. Suddenly she was in his arms, her whole body trembling.

"Oh, Richard, hold me tight! Please hold me tight! I've never known what it's like to be terrified before."

The knowledge that she depended upon him, that she needed his protection, replaced his own panic by a matter-of-fact courage, an unbelievable calmness.

"Ann, darling, whatever it is, we're in it together. Together, we can face it—and knock hell out of it, maybe."

She clung to him fiercely. "Why did I ever send you away?"

"No matter what happens, remember I love you, Ann. I'll go on loving you. I'll love you forever."

Blindly she sought his lips.

But at that moment the whole house seemed to rock from a subtle impact, all the walls and furniture—everything billowed like slack painted canvas on a drafty stage. Then the humming came, so loud that it seemed to resonate in flesh and bone; seemed to oscillate drunkenly along every separate nerve while making its dark, fatal progress to the citadel of the brain.

The crescendo gathered; and Sheridan, supporting Ann with all his strength, knew that nothing could stand against it. Knew that the terrible whirlwind of sound could shake the life out of their bodies in the space of a single heartbeat. Dumbly he realized there was no end to it—just as there could never have been a beginning.

Then the climax came—a moment when the world seemed to unstitch, when the entire cosmos became translucent, and he could see a fantastic sweep of day-hidden stars blossom

61

brilliantly then fade into a uniform darkness. Time had lost its meaning, but Sheridan could still be vaguely surprised that it took so long to die. He was already conditioned to destruction, and so the last trick came as the greatest shock of all.

Suddenly the universe was switched on again. Darkness was swallowed by light; the house floated back into existence; stillness froze the shimmering stage canvas into a new reality.

Sheridan found it hard to believe that he was still holding Ann in his arms—hard to believe that she, to, was still alive.

She opened her eyes. They were cold, remote, drained of all emotion. Even fear. She registered the textbook symptoms of extreme shock.

"That machine," she whispered sleepily. "That damned experiment!" Without any warning she fainted.

Sheridan carried her, found a divan in one of the rooms and laid her gently on it. He saw a decanter and glasses on a small table. The decanter was half full of whisky. Holding it with difficulty, he poured two generous measures, slopping the stuff all over the table.

As he picked up the glasses Ann came around. He gave one to her. "Drink it slowly. . . . I'd better go up to the lab and see if he's all right." He gulped his own whisky, and was glad to feel the burning down his throat.

"I—I'll come with you," said Ann, shakily trying to get up.

"No you won't. You'll stay here till I get back. Not a move —understand?"

She nodded abjectly. "I just don't want to be . . . alone."

"Darling, I must find out what's happened."

"Yes, I know."

"I'l only be three or four minutes—less, maybe."

Ann tried to smile. "I'll be waiting," she said.

Sheridan kissed her lightly, then nerved himself to investigate.

The whisky had induced a certain recklessness. He took the flight of stairs two at a time; and when he reached the top level his heart was pounding.

There he hesitated a moment before he remembered which way to turn. Then a dozen steps along a dim, narrow passage brought him to the lab door.

He began to panic again, and knew why. There was absolute silence. For a slow and painful minute his mind and body became the battleground in a silent civil war. Instinct told him to get out, run away, escape—do anything but go ahead. Reason told him to turn the handle and enter. He waited quietly, wondering what he would do. But the tension became more than he could bear.

Suddenly he ended it. He turned the handle, threw open the door and took a step forward. He tried to turn back too late.

There was no laboratory, no time machine, no sign of Professor Robert Blackmore. There was nothing!

Except a maelstrom of darkness . . . a shaft of infinite depth . . . a tunnel, cut clean through the thin fabric of time!

Even as he fell, even as the dark pool sucked him down, he remembered Ann's last words:

"I'll be waiting," she had said.

Then there was nothing left to remember, nothing at all. . . .

Sheridan woke up suddenly with a faint, high-pitched humming in his ears—like the sound of a remote machine. Immediately, he knew there was a dream he should try to remember, a dream that had some terrible bearing on reality. . . .

THE BRAIN CHILD

Though Dr. Thomas Merrinoe quietly deplored the fact that his ten-year-old son showed no sign of being a genius, he was thankful for small mercies. The boy did not possess two heads, nor was he a congenital idiot in the clinical sense. Objectively, it might almost be said that Timothy was a normal specimen—with, perhaps, a rather generous share of atavistic traits.

This was a source of continual wonder to Dr. Merrinoe. As the director of a team engaged in designing and building electronic brains he was professionally shocked to think that even such an inferior calculator as a human being could be manufactured by unskilled labor. Fortunately or otherwise this did not prevent him from begetting Timothy.

But as a fond father Dr. Merrinoe fell somewhat short of the conventional standard. His wife, Mary, a sensible blonde who regarded trigonometry as a serious abdominal operation, had much difficulty in persuading him that babyhood and infancy were not only desirable but necessary. With characteristic impatience Dr. Merrinoe had hoped to teach young Timothy chess at the age of three and differential calculus by four and a half.

After all, he argued, what was the use of science if it could not be applied to life? If it was possible to program an electronic brain for all processes of mathematical reasoning, why could not the same thing be done to a small boy? He found the answer very quickly. It was tragically simple. In the matter of learning the machine had no option; the boy had!

By the time he was ten Timothy had not only managed to destroy Dr. Merrinoe's faith in every known method of education and driven him to seek consolation in bigger and better electronic brains, he had also managed to ignore the science of mathematics *in toto* and completely.

Thus at the very apex of Dr. Merrinoe's career when, after three years of unremitting labor, he had brought to completion the electronic brain called Peeping Tom, the fruits of victory tasted slightly sour.

He had built a brain that could see, hear, speak and—in a limited sense—feel. He had built a brain that could make any other electronic bird cage in the Western world look foolish. He had programed Peeping Tom to answer questions that nobody was clever enough to ask. Yet he could not teach his own son that half of a half was a quarter.

Sitting one afternoon in front of Peeping Tom's chromium-plated face, staring at his television screen eyes and his loudspeaker mouth, Dr. Merrinoe felt no elation at all—only a faint bitterness. It was, he thought, a matter of regret that you could work out blueprints for practically everything except babies.

Recently he had acquired the habit of talking to himself, fortunately only when he was alone. But though his present reverie was no more than a quietly mumbled monologue he was soon reminded that he was not quite alone.

"I beg your pardon, sir," boomed Peeping Tom, "but would you kindly state the precise terms of reference?"

Dr. Merrinoe blushed guiltily, then remembered that Peeping Tom was only a machine, after all. "Go to blazes, you great glorified pianola! I wasn't talking to you."

"Sorry, sir," returned Peeping Tom abjectly, "but as there appears to be no one else present, and since you programed me to tackle all questions, I concluded—"

"Switch yourself off,' interrupted the physicist. "Go to sleep."

Peeping Tom's eyes glowed reproachfully. "Yes, sir."

"No, wait a minute!" snapped Merrinoe. "Are you intelligent?"

"No, sir. Merely clever."

"Correct. Now tell me who made you, who owns you and what you're worth."

"You designed me, sir, and your team constructed me. I'm owned by *Imperial Electric Inc.*, who paid two million, two hundred and forty-five thousand, three hundred and sixty-seven dollars and thirty-three cents for materials and construction."

"That's right," agreed Dr. Merrinoe. "Can you beat me at chess?"

"Yes, sir."

"Can you calculate how many atoms there are in the cosmos?"

"Yes, sir—approximately."

"Can you work out how much rice the probable population of China will consume in 1975?"

"Yes, sir."

"Then," said Dr. Merrinoe with irony, "you will doubtless be able to solve a comparatively simple problem. Why does a baby suck its thumb?" He sat back complacently, waiting for Peeping Tom to admit defeat.

"A baby sucks its thumb," replied the brain unexpectedly, "for the following reasons: a) because it is weaned too early, b) because it is teething, c) because it experiences insecurity, or d) because it is hungry. If thumb-sucking persists it is recommended that—"

"I'll be darned!" said Dr. Merrinoe. "Who programed you with that stuff?"

Peeping Tom seemed to enjoy his moment of triumph. "You did, sir," he purred. "During the first test programing series, you arranged for me to store the contents of a thousand assorted handbooks in my memory banks. One of them was *Baby and Child Care* by Benjamin Spock, M.D."

Dr. Merrinoe was slightly furious. "Well, then, you ampere-sucking incubus, perhaps you will kindly tell me why my son, Timothy combines the physical characteristics of *homo sapiens* with the mental ability of an anthropoid ape?"

"According to the theory of evolution," began Peeping Tom sententiously, "a primitive life-form is capable of—"

"Beating your dull-witted circuits out with a large monkey wrench," interrupted the physicist, childishly indulging a much repressed desire to be rude. "Now allow me to rephrase the question. Why is my son intellectually retarded, in spite of his general background?"

"May I request relevant data?"

"Proceed," said Dr. Merrinoe regally. "I will endeavour to be quite objective."

Despite his mechanical limitations, Peeping Tom contrived

65

to give the impression of one drawing a deep breath. "I require to know his age, weight, height, physical type, shape of skull, approximate vocabulary, manual attainments, emotional characteristics, primary interests, habits, hobbies and ambitions. I also need to evaluate his relationship with his mother, and his relationship with you."

Dr. Merrinoe gazed at Peeping Tom's wall-length face, awestruck. "You don't want much, do you?"

"No, sir," agreed Peeping Tom blandly. Then he added: "If I may make a suggestion, sir, why not tell me about Timothy in your own way? I will marshal the relevant facts as they emerge."

Dr. Merrinoe was too immersed in the proposition to realize that a tremendous milestone in the history of electronic computers had just been passed. It was the first time one had ever made a suggestion on its own initiative.

"As I see it," began the physicist thoughtfully, "Timothy has one outstanding quality—stubbornness. He's as stubborn as a mule with a carrot complex. At first I told myself it was only a sort of sturdy independence, but . . ." And he went on and on, talking through half the afternoon, confiding his problems to the machine of his own creation. Peeping Tom listened quietly, his square eyes dull with the deceptive somnolence of a fat cubist owl.

Finally Dr. Merrinoe appeared to have exhausted himself. He broke off in the middle of a sentence whose point he had already forgotten, blinked foolishly and came to the conclusion that he had recently been working too hard.

Peeping Tom seized the opportunity to deliver his verdict: "The available evidence, sir, points clearly to maladjustment. However, there is—"

"Maladjustment!" snorted Dr. Merrinoe. "Of course the boy's maladjusted. That's what I've been wasting my time telling you."

Peeping Tom's eyes glowed brightly. "I do not mean that Timothy is a maladjusted child," he announced. "But you, sir, seem to be a maladjusted parent."

Dr. Merrinoe tried to preserve a tiny shred of scientific detachment. "An interesting theory," he conceded, with some irony. "Naturally you have a solution to offer . . ."

"Naturally," agreed Peeping Tom. "Since you have failed to arouse the boy's intellectual curiosity it follows that a different stimulus should be applied."

"What?" inquired Dr. Merrinoe.

"Me," replied Peeping Tom.

Dr. Merrinoe closed the front door quietly behind him and managed to raise a tired smile for his wife.

"Had a good day, darling?" asked Mary.

He noted with satisfaction that, at thirty-seven, she was still uncommonly attractive. It was a great consolation.

"Terrible," he answered. "We've now got to the stage where the brain talks back. . . . . How about a nice passionate kiss?"

"Make it eighty per cent nice and twenty per cent passionate," she said. "Dinner is in a critical condition."

He duly translated the wild impulse of abandon into a restrained domestic clinch.

"Where's Timothy?" he inquired casually.

"Watching some cloak-and-dagger stuff on television."

Dr. Merrinoe made a noise like a punctured tire. "I've got a good mind to take an axe to that damned box of tricks. It's ruining his initiative, to say nothing of his critical faculty. When I was his age—"

"Darling," interrupted Mrs. Merrinoe gently, "you're using up too much adrenaline. I do wish you'd control your language a little more—at home, anyway. Little somethings have big ears."

"Humph! Has Wonder Boy dined?"

"Yes, he didn't want to miss the play."

"He didn't want to miss the play!" echoed Dr. Merrinoe irritably, following his wife into the dining room. "Well, I suppose we ought to be thankful for a quiet meal together, anyway. Incidentally, I want to have a little chat with him afterwards. . . . Do I smell something burning?"

Mary sighed. "Only yourself, dear. Look, why don't you see a psychiatrist?"

"About Timothy?"

"No, about you. Timothy's all right, but he seems to be giving you a king-size anxiety neurosis. If you left him alone we'd all get along far better."

"Anxiety neurosis! The boy can't even tell me what the square root of eighty-one is without behaving like a contortionist."

"Neither can I."

Dr. Merrinoe tried to register a superior and at the same time lecherous smile. "I didn't marry you for your brains, darling."

"And I," retorted his wife drily, "did not conceive Timothy for his. Now don't argue; it's bad for your digestion."

Dr. Merrinoe did not argue. He stared at the plate in front of him and brooded. It was all very well for Mary to dismiss the boy's intellectual weakness so lightly: those who have beauty do not usually concern themselves overmuch with brainpower. But while Mary's purpose in life was chiefly decorative, her son's definitely wasn't.

The trouble with Timothy, thought Dr. Merrinoe wearily, was that he didn't have very much of anything. His personality was nonedescript; and though he certainly wasn't ugly his features had a vague impression of being thrown together hurriedly—as if their creator had just been putting on the finishing touches when the lunch whistle blew.

At last, when Dr. Merrinoe had simmered down and was lingering over his second cup of coffee and a cigarette, the object of this sad reverie deigned to put in an appearance.

"Hi, Dad," said Timothy, peering cautiously around the door.

"Hello, son," said Dr. Merrinoe, coaxing his face into what was meant to be a friendly smile.

Placing a more reasonable interpretation on the expression, Timothy advanced and tried to make his voice sound sympathetic: "Have you got neuralgia again?"

"No, I haven't got neuralgia," retorted his father irritably. "Whatever makes you think that?"

"Nothing."

"Then don't be an idiot. . . . Did you enjoy the play?"

"It was passable. I wish they'd do another about space flight, though."

"If you're interested in space flight," began Dr. Merrinoe diplomatically, "how would you like to be able to work out the escape velocity of a moon rocket?"

"Not very much, thank you. I'd rather build one."

"You can't build one until you know enough math to—"

Timothy yawned. "That's why I'd rather watch it on television." His father began to look as if he had neuralgia again, only worse.

"Timothy," said Dr. Merrinoe gently, "how would you like to come with me tomorrow and see Peeping Tom?"

"That old brain you've been throwing together?"

"Yes."

"Oh. . . . Tomorrow's Saturday, isn't it?"

"It is. Does that make any difference?"

Timothy took a deep breath. "I was hoping to go to the movies."

Dr. Merrinoe likewise took a deep breath. "You're going to see the brain."

Mrs. Merrinoe gave her husband a glance of intense exasperation. It was a look that told him he would be in for a rough half hour when Timothy had gone to bed.

On Saturday afternoon a tall man and a small boy threaded their way through the vast weekend necropolis of Imperial Electric Inc. Dr. Merrinoe, with a mixture of curiosity and resignation, led Timothy, with a mixture of resignation and curiosity, among the coppery maze of spider webs where Peeping Tom sat spinning his electronic dreams.

They climbed up a narrow staircase and entered the control room. Dr. Merrinoe pressed the master-switch, and Peeping Tom's eyes glowed drowsily. Timothy was mildly impressed.

"I am alert, sir," said Peeping Tom. "What are your instructions?"

Dr. Merrinoe settled Timothy in the audience chair.

"I shall leave my son, Timothy, here while I finish some work in my office. You will answer any questions he may ask, and generaly keep him amused until I return."

"Yes, sir," boomed Peeping Tom.

Dr. Merrinoe could have sworn that the brain managed to wink. As he went downstairs again he heard Timothy's opening gambit:

"If one and half squirrels atc one and a half nuts in one and a half days, how many nuts would nine squirrels eat in nine days?"

"Eighty-one," murmured the physicist absently to himself, then shot a startled glance over his shoulder as he heard the brain say: "Fifty-four, sir."

For the next couple of hours Dr. Merrinoe sat in his office and was entirely absorbed in a science-fiction pulp magazine. Eventually he looked at the desk clock, and was suddenly jerked back from a world where amphibious octopods pursued beautiful Earth girls and almost caught them.

Two solid hours! He'd only meant to leave Timothy for forty-five minutes or so!

Dr. Merrinoe hastily dropped the pulp magazine in his "in" basket, then rushed out of the office and headed for the control room with some apprehension. It was all very well to let Peeping Tom attempt to improve Timothy, but what if Timothy had attempted to improve Peeping Tom?

As, with beating heart, he ran up the stairs, Dr. Merrinoe heard noise that sounded like the world's champion fast-talker limbering up in Chinese. But even as he opened the door the screech slowed down until it became recognizable. A staccato volley marked the end of Peeping Tom's high-pressure discourse. Timothy was fast asleep. Dr. Merrinoe felt a wave of relief.

"The experiment seems to have produced a negative result," he remarked, staring at his gently snoring son.

"Merely a deep-level hypnosis, sir," explained Peeping Tom. "It was necessary to bypass the inhibiting factors before I could program him adequately."

"Before you could *what?*" Dr. Merrinoe gaped.

"Before I could program him adequately. He has now received an advance course in mathematics and physics. I trust you will find the result satisfactory."

"There's just one small point," said Dr. Merrinoe, breathing heavily, "my son, you dim-witted squawk-box is not a machine."

"No, sir," agreed Peeping Tom. "Therefore I allowed for a seventy per cent inefficiency. Perhaps you would care to waken him gently?"

The physicist did so. After a few moments Timothy opened his eyes, yawned and stretched. "Very interesting," he remarked vaguely, "but can we go home now? I'm hungry."

Dr. Merrinoe treated the electronic brain to a pitying smile. But Peeping Tom made no comment—being, apparently in a mood to hibernate.

The first reaction occurred after an unusually quiet tea. Instead of glueing himself to the television, Timothy disappeared into his father's study to emerge several minutes later with a book. He then found a quiet corner, settled himself and began to read.

"You've been bullying him," accused Mary in a whisper. "What went on this afternoon?"

"Nothing," said Dr. Merrinoe uncomfortably. "Nothing at all. I just left him to amuse himself with Peeping Tom while I cleared up some paperwork."

"Well, *somebody* has been bullying him," she insisted. "Or else he's feeling ill."

Timothy looked up from his novel. "Do you think a man could make himself invisible?" he asked.

"Certainly not," replied his father. "Why?"

"That's what this book is about, *The Invisible Man*. It looks a pretty good story."

Remembering his own H. G. Wells period, Dr. Merrinoe

was surprised. "Isn't it a little too hard for you, Timothy? *I* didn't read it until I was fourteen or so."

Timothy smiled. "It's old-fashioned, but I can manage. . . . How would you like a game of chess, Dad? We haven't played for some time."

Dr. Merrinoe felt slightly uneasy. "I thought you didn't like chess. You used to say it bored you."

"It did," said Timothy blandly. "But I was younger then." He rubbed his freckled forehead and looked puzzled for a moment. Then he went to a small bureau, took out the chessmen and board and began to set up the pieces. He grinned pleasantly at his father.

"I think I'll watch television," said Mrs. Merrinoe faintly, "while you two geniuses fight it out."

Dr. Merrinoe looked at her, gave a helpless shrug, then turned his attention to the chess board.

"Would you be angry if I beat you?" demanded Timothy.

"Certainly not," snapped Dr. Merrinoe, opening with his king's pawn. "I should be very glad indeed—also surprised."

"I shouldn't," said Timothy.

But after fifteen minutes his father checkmated him easily —with a feeling of relief. The boy had not changed—or very little, anyway.

"You weren't playing your best," accused Timothy.

"I beat you, didn't I?"

A crafty smile flickered over Timothy's face. "Let's have another game. I'd forgotten some of the gambits."

"Thirsting for revenge?" said Dr. Merrinoe dryly. He set up the pieces again.

Timothy frowned slightly, then said with some hesitation, "Would you give me fifteen dollars if I win?"

"*What!*"

"I said, would you give me fifteen dollars if I win?"

Dr. Merrinoe regarded his son gravely. "And what do I get if *I* win?"

"Thirty cents a week for a year," said Timothy promptly. "That's fair, isn't it?"

"I think so," answered his father, with a thin smile. "I hope this is going to be a lesson for you. Why do you want fifteen dollars?"

Timothy grinned. "I'll tell you after the game."

"Your move," said Dr. Merrinoe grimly.

It lasted slightly more than two hours, and proved to be quite a classic. At first Dr. Merrinoe moved carelessly, then with more caution. After twenty minutes he lost a knight and a bishop in rapid succession, while Timothy merely sacrificed three pawns.

This seemed to unnerve the physicist. He began to play with deathly concentration until a sudden stroke of brilliance that should have given him the game somehow cost him his queen.

Meanwhile Timothy had taken to reading his novel between moves. Almost regretfully he administered the *coup de grace,* at the same time reaching the end of chapter seventeen.

"Timothy," said Dr. Merrinoe in a cracked voice, as he reached for his billfold, "how did you do it?"

"Just followed the pattern," replied the boy enigmatically.

There was a profound silence while Timothy collected his winnings and, after a careful recount, pocketed the dollar bills. His father stared anxiously at this pint-sized Frankenstein that was his own flesh and blood.

Eventually Dr. Merrinoe was moved to consider the purpose behind this sinister confidence trick. "What are you going to do with the money?" he demanded.

"Buy a few things I need for some experiments."

"I see," said Dr. Merrinoe blindly.

Timothy yawned. "I think Ill go to bed now. Thanks for the games, Dad. I hope you didn't mind losing."

"Not at all," grated his father. "It was a pleasure."

Mrs. Merrinoe, whose interest in television had fallen to zero from the moment Timothy began to win, watched her small retreating son with awe. She noticed that the copy of *The Invisible Man* was tucked firmly under his arm.

When he had closed the door behind him she pounced on her husband like a broody lioness. "Wha's happened to my little boy?" she demanded. "What have you done to him?"

"Nothing—nothing at all," he said helplessly. "I expect Peeping Tom taught him a few tricks, but they'll soon wear off."

"Wear off!" snapped Mary. "I should hope so—for your sake! If that electronic egg-timer's done any harm to Timothy, I'll . . . I'll . . ." She froze him with an angry glare

Remembering Peeping Tom's hypnotic programing, Dr. Merrinoe winced.

For the rest of the weekend, there was a somewhat uneasy armistice. Unconsciously Dr. Merrinoe avoided his son as much as possible, while Timothy, for his part, spent a great deal of time in his own room.

The physicist discovered that a few more books had disappeared from his study, including one massive tome on wave mechanics. The thought of Timothy reading up on wave mechanics was no longer ridiculous, it was terrifying. But he made no comment, thinking it wiser to await results.

He did not have to wait long.

The storm broke on Monday evening. Returning home late after a long and unrewarding experiment Dr. Merrinoe was confronted by a hysterical wife.

"Thank heaven you've arrived!" she sobbed. "I've been trying to call you for the last hour. You've got to do something about Timothy *quickly*, before I go out of my mind!"

"Timothy?" echoed Dr. Merrinoe nervously. "Where is he? Is he all right?"

"All right!" shrieked Mrs. Merrinoe. "You'll see if he's all right!"

At that moment the dining room door opened and a pair of shoes walked down the hall. They were inhabited by an empty pair of stockings which invisibly supported a small boy's vacant suit.

"Hi, Dad," said Timothy cheerfully. "I wanted to give you a surprise."

Dr. Merrinoe cringed from the apparition. "Timothy," he croaked, "Timothy! What have you done?"

"Rearranged my molecular structure," replied Timothy calmly, "and lowered my refractive index to zero."

"It's—it's—it's impossible!"

"You said that before but, well, here I am. The man in the book did it, and so have I."

The sweat dripped from Dr. Merrinoe's forehead. "But Timothy, listen! The book was only a story—fiction. It just couldn't happen."

"It has," said Timothy. "Feel my hand." He prodded his father, not too gently, underneath the ribs. "Would you say that was fiction?"

Dr. Merrinoe coughed and sat down suddenly, his legs giving way like overloaded pit props. Mrs. Merrinoe, having now reached breaking point, fainted and with excellent timing slid gently into her husband's arms.

"Now see what you've done," he panted angrily. "We'd better get her onto the couch." As he struggled with his wife's limp form Dr. Merrinoe was helped by a pair of invisible hands.

He settled her in a relaxed position, then turned pathetically to the vacant suit. "How—did you—"

"The apparatus is in my room," said Timothy. Anticipating

73

his father's next move, he added, "No, don't go there. You may get electrocuted, or turn invisible. or something. From now on my room will have to be private."

Dr. Merrinoe was about to lay down the law, but thought better of it. "All right, son," he said meekly. "But Timothy —can you—can you change back?"

There was childish laughter. "I don't want to. This is fun. Besides, think what they'll say at school."

Dr. Merrinoe shuddered. He was thinking what the world might say. He was also thinking what the world might possibly *do*. At that moment Mary opened her eyes. She looked as if she was getting ready to scream. It was the last straw. Dr. Merrinoe panicked.

"Timothy, you've got to change back," he pleaded. "You've *got* to. It's not decent. It's . . ." He floundered, inwardly praying for spiritual guidance. How could he ever hope to control an invisible boy?

Then suddenly Dr. Merrinoe was inspired. "I'll bet you twenty-five dollars," he said sadly, "that you can't become visible again."

"Done!" snapped Timothy. Suit, stockings and shoes galvanized into action. A door opened and slammed, and the invisible boy bounded upstairs three at a time. With an abject sigh Dr. Merrinoe turned to his wife and patted her hand reassuringly.

"I'll divorce you," she hissed. "For extreme cruelty. You and that psychopathic brain!"

"Now, Mary," he soothed. "It's going to work out all right. We'll just have to watch him carefully for a while."

"Watch him carefully!" she stormed. "When at any moment he might decide to turn us into a couple of white mice."

"It's not as bad as that, dear. If you understood a little physics I could—"

"Physics!" she scoffed. "Can *you* make yourself invisible? Don't be a moron." She dabbed at her eyes with a handkerchief and sniffed. "It's the work of the Devil."

Unless the Devil had also been programed by Peeping Tom, Dr. Merrinoe doubted that he would have enough scientific knowledge to be of practical assistance. But Mary was in no mood for reasonable discussion, so he let it pass.

He would have given anything to watch Timothy making himself visible again, but somehow that didn't seem advisable. He sat down and waited tensely.

A mysterious humming started upstairs. It sounded like a

muffled hornet. Presently it changed into a high-pitched whirring that died slowly into silence. Then there was a sound like breaking glass.

A few moments later Timothy came back into the room, wearing a benign smile on his chubby, substantial face. Dr. Merrinoe mopped his forehead. Then he saw the purposeful gleam in Timothy's eye, and hastily took out his billfold. He selected a five and two tens.

"Now, Timothy," he waved them slowly in front of the boy's nose, "I want you to promise that you'll never make anyone or anything invisible with that—that apparatus. In fact, it would be a good thing if we took it to pieces tonight. Of course I'll just take a few notes for the sake of a scientific record, but—"

"Nobody goes into my room," interrupted Timothy decisively. His hand close around the bills. "Now that I've done it once I'm beginning to lose interest. I only worked on it because you said it was impossible. But I've just discovered a far more interesting problem."

"What's that?" squeaked Dr. Merrinoe in top falsetto.

"Anti-gravity," said Timothy with a happy smile.

Dr. Merrinoe experienced an odd darkness descending. The room began to sway slightly, and he had a vague feeling that presently the floor would rise up and hit him.

From far, far away, he heard Timothy eagerly explaining why the general theory of relativity was just a little unsound. But Dr. Merrinoe was more concerned with the practical side. He was already figuring how much it would cost him *not* to go to the moon.

FALCON CHASE

Nine days afterward, when the machine and the bodies had long ago been claimed by the scientists; when the official reports had been typed out, dispatched—and pigeonholed; when the last journalist had drifted away, dully resentful at having got only the *beginning* of the scoop of the century; nine days afterward, when the incident was already a legend, the three men met to discuss it—each wishing to be convinced by the others that the whole thing was real.

Their cars stood outside The Green Man, a quiet inn six miles out of town on the Falconford road. Nine days ago The Green Man had developed the tense atmosphere of a battle headquarters. But now, the excitement was dying—even the landlord was voicing opinions less frequently—and the three men were able, for the first time, to think about it leisurely and in peace.

Sir Alan Leclerc, the chief constable, listened to Inspector Manning as to an equal; while Major Nore sipped his whisky and tried to picture the kind of warfare which once belonged to the more sensational children's comics.

The September twilight deepened. Presently they lost their embarrassment in the intimate glow of a single oil lamp which softened the Best Room of The Green Man into a lazy ring of shadows. Presently, the men who had dealt solely with facts began to enter the realm of conjecture.

Toward midnight on September 9th a brilliant green shooting star made its appearance remote in the North African sky. It was first seen at Ain Sefra. Later, during the early hours of the morning, it was observed over the Algerian coast, and then the Mediterranean. But unlike most shooting stars, this one did not disappear after a moment or two. Instead, it moved at a high speed in wide circles, yet all the time progressing slowly north. As dawn came nearer, the shooting star was seen above Valencia, Bordeaux, Havre and, finally, London.

Then daybreak came, a gray reluctant ghost.

Meanwhile, the alarm bell had sounded at Redmoor Hall Settlement, a large country house which recently had been converted for the accommodation and treatment of criminal lunatics. It was the first time a patient had escaped.

Two hours later, those inhabitants of East Anglia who had switched on their radios heard the eight o'clock news bulletin rapidly become swamped by a sound something like a fast approaching motorboat.

Later reports showed that the interference had been noticed as far north as Dundee.

At ten minutes past eight, the "motorboating" ceased to interfere with radio reception. At the same time, the people of Cambridge were aware of a brief penetrating hiss, as an indistinguishable but blinding streak of light swept over the city. It was followed by a faintly acrid scent and, a minute or so later, by a miniature whirlwind.

In peaceful fields along the Norfolk border, forty head of placid cattle stampeded. They flattened the hedges and charged along the lanes, to finish up entirely exhausted; some with broken legs and ripped udders.

At quarter-past eight, the county police, under the able

76

direction of Inspector Manning, had thrown a patrolling cordon round the four square miles of forest that was Falcon Chase. The inspector, a seasoned hunter of men, hoped to recapture the maniac before midday. He was in a hurry to return to his Norwich burglary; and he was also annoyed that the army, which was using the Chase for an exercise, should have offered to help in the search.

Major Nore was enthusiastic. He gleefully informed the four platoons detailed for the operation that George William Grandiman, besides being a specialist in the destruction of children, was equally expert in the murder of adults. Major Nore also indicated that it was up to the army to recapture Grandiman before the police did. Major Nore also added that he wished the prisoner to be taken alive and uninjured.

The police and the soldiers had begun to close in, truncheons drawn, rifles at the ready but unloaded. The walkie-talkies kept up their monotonous, parrot-wise signals of progress. All this was ordinary procedure for this out-of-the-ordinary job.

But then extraordinary things began to happen.

Major Nore and Inspector Manning, who were busy being consciously polite to each other, were taken unawares by the same blinding flash of light and the loud hiss that had been noticed over Cambridge. The light was lower and brighter, the hiss louder. The consequent whirlwind was more powerful.

A radio operator, standing six or seven yards away from Inspector Manning, seemed to make without any effort the jump of a lifetime. He rose forty feet in the air and sailed majestically into the branches of a great oak. He stayed there, hanging in the fork of a thick branch, quite unconscious.

Inspector Manning's respectable black police car was lifted by invisible fingers, turned neatly over and deposited in the middle of the by-road with a depressing crunch. Major Nore's heavy olive-colored sedan, in spite of its handbrake, was backed into a four foot ditch.

An army dispatch rider, traveling at fifty miles an hour along the Falconford road, had the frightening experience of being stopped suddenly by an unseen force. He was later found, unable to speak.

The inspector and the major were fortunate enough merely to suffer the indignity of being flattened. When the whirlwind had passed them they lifted their heads and gazed around at the hundreds of trees almost completely stripped of their leaves. At that moment there was a far sound of shattering timbers, and a great wall of flame seemed to hover for a moment, a quarter of a mile away, above the treetops of Falcon Chase.

The inspector and the major looked at each other. This was no time for theories. Major Nore ran to his car, wrenched open the door and hauled out a spare walkie-talkie.

In less than a minute, two platoons of men were moving at the double toward the part of the forest where the flames had been seen.

Thoughts of George William Grandiman and his imminent recapture were eclipsed in Inspector Manning's mind as he raced after the major. With a twinge of self-contempt, he realized that the automatic pistol in his hand was a definite comfort.

"What the devil is it?" he panted.

Major Nore stopped for a moment and tried to control his own heavy breathing: "R.A.F. up to some damn thing, I expect. Not surprised at anything nowadays, with all this jet stuff. . . . Better push on, and see if there are any survivors!"

"Did you see anything like a plane?" asked the inspector.

"No," snorted the major, "but I damn well felt it! Same noise, same smell—recognize it anywhere!"

"It made a mess of my car."

"It made a mess of my signaler," said the Major dryly. "Come on! It's not far now."

They sprinted along between the trees and arrived at the scene a few minutes before the two platoons that had been diverted by Major Nore.

Luckily the forest was very damp after a period of heavy rainfall, and the sudden wall of flame that had been seen by the two men had now died down. It had obviously not started among the closely growing trees, for the boles of those that were still standing were damp and unscarred, while their branches and foliage were black and shriveled.

An astounding sight met their eyes.

An avenue about two hundred yards long and twenty yards wide had been carved out of the living forest. Dozens of trees had been flattened or bent forward, their roots torn from the earth, as if they were so many matchsticks. At the end of this avenue, its nose buried in earth and broken branches, lay what at first appeared to be a huge silver bullet. It was about ninety feet long and twenty feet in diameter.

Standing in silent amazement behind this extraordinary object, Inspector Manning and Major Nore saw that its rear was a mass of twisted and dully glowing metal tubes. A slight breeze caused something at the side of the machine to move. It appeared to be some kind of door.

"Come on," said the inspector grimly. "Your guess is as good as mine. I think I've seen too many strip cartoons lately!" He walked slowly and purposefully toward the open door, gripping his automatic tightly.

Major Nore followed without comment, his hand firmly holding the butt of his service pistol.

At the door they paused.

"This is giving me the creeps. I wonder if there's—anyone at home?" Major Nore was surprised to hear that his own voice had dropped to a whisper.

"Even if there is I shouldn't think they'll be full of joy after a bump like this," replied the inspector quietly. "What do you say—shall we go in, or sing out to them first?"

"Wish my men would hurry up," said the major anxiously. Then, with characteristic decision, he moved ahead of the inspector and scrambled up through the doorway.

The interior was not unlike that of a super trailer—what the salesmen would call "a functional-living van"—except that the materials were strange, the design better, and everything was much smaller.

There were four bunks—each not more than four feet long—which were independently slung from a kind of delicate spider's web of metal. But the metal felt and responded like tough elastic. By the side of each bunk was a panel of switches and instruments, and on the bunk itself a number of thin silver straps. Altogether, the arrangement was a masterly example of shock absorption. Major Nore felt that traveling in them would be rather like lying on three spring mattresses aboard a stratocruiser.

It was only when he had spent thirty or forty seconds gazing about him that he realized there was no source of light. But everything glowed faintly—while contriving not to be luminous. It was as if the quality of light itself had been trapped in the materials of the bunks, the tiny fixed tables and chairs, and all the strange gadgets in the rear compartment. The effect was startling, but pleasant. It was as if the whole cabin were illuminated by some highly developed form of indirect lighting.

The major heard Inspector Manning's voice from outside: "You all right, Major? Anyone on board?"

"Come and have a look," called the major.

Cautiously, Inspector Manning clambered through the doorway.

"Now we've found something for the clever boys to think about!" remarked the major lightly. As he spoke his gaze traveled past the astonished inspector to the nose of the compartment. It was cut off from the rest of the machine by a partition of what looked to be glass. With a stifled exclamation he gripped the inspector's arm and pointed.

The nose compartment was obviously the control room. There were instruments everywhere: large clocks (bearing no terrestrial figures); things like thermometers; a battery of differently colored switches and buttons; and three large vision screens. In front of the central control panel was an adjustable couch. Across it was sprawled the body of what seemed to be a fair-haired human child.

The two men tried to enter the nose compartment, but the transparent sliding door was jammed. They could only gaze and conjecture. The "child" was dressed in a flimsy kind of knee-length tunic. It reminded Inspector Manning of the illustrations that are sometimes found in Latin schoolbooks.

"It looks as if his neck's broken." The inspector felt the need to break an uneasy silence.

Major Nore tried desperately to regain a sense of proportion—earthly proportion: "I'll bet the Wright brothers didn't count on anything like this!" He gave a brief, rather forced laugh. He caught the inspector's expression and suddenly became serious.

"This is certainly going to be one big headache for the government. . . . I wonder where it came from?"

"Well, he can't tell us now." The inspector jerked his head toward the still figure. "We'll have to try and get hold of his companions. . . . They seem to have been in quite a hurry to explore. How long did it take us to get here?"

"Ten minutes," said the major. "Probably less. You don't think there are more of them wandering about the Chase?"

The inspector nodded. "Unless they're hiding in cupboards," he said without humor. "Somehow, I don't think this one would have fancied the trip by himself. And there are the bunks. . . ."

Major Nore was completed at a loss. "It's made a mess of your manhunt," was all he could find to say.

"From singular to plural," said the inspector briefly.

The major thought about that. Then he said: "I say, Manning. It's sort of comforting to know they—they're human."

"And little humans, at that," added the inspector with a thin smile.

There were sounds outside. One of the major's platoons had

arrived. He immediately got out of the machine and became very military.

"What is it, Major?" The voice of the young "sub" in charge of the men was filled with excitement and wonder.

"Later!" snapped the major. "Look here, Carlslake, I want your men to throw a cordon round this—contrivance. Nobody enters—understand!"

"Yes, sir." Carslake was crestfallen.

"Inspector Manning and I are going to take a look around. Keep position till we come back. . . . Oh, and when Willow's platoon arrives, tell them to begin searching from here—in concentric circles. . . . Tell him—tell him to look for a couple of children—Roman children—as well as Grandiman!"

A constable came running breathlessly between the trees. He stopped still for a moment, his mouth dropping open. Then duty asserted itself, and he made for the inspector.

"The army reports contacting Grandiman, sir. But he bashed one of the soldiers and ran for it."

"Where's this?" asked the inspector sharply.

"South side, sir—two miles away."

"Look here. Get to the nearest phone and get hold of the chief constable. Ask him to come here as soon as he can. It's urgent."

"Yes, sir." The constable moved away at a tired jog-trot.

Inspector Manning turned to the major. "We'd better get moving." He gazed speculatively at the great machine behind them. "I rather think I'd like to be in at the first meeting between us and *them*."

Major Nore tried to take the whole thing in his stride. "A good idea," he grunted breezily. "Be something to tell our grandchildren, eh, Manning?"

"If we have any," was the laconic reply.

But it was a man from Willow's platoon who discovered them first. Major Nore and the inspector, picking their way gingerly among the bracken, heard a great shout of surprise. Then a private came running toward them down a narrow avenue between pine trees.

"Found 'em, sir," he yelled to Major Nore. "Come and have a look!"

The major, who was equally excited, did not stop to discuss the finer points of discipline. It wouldn't have been much use, anyway, for the private, a raw lad, had already turned around and was charging back to a small clearing. Major Nore cast his official dignity to the winds, and took off in pursuit. But the inspector stood there for a few moments, considering the happenings of the past twenty minutes, before he followed.

Major Nore and the private had already disturbed the bodies.

The inspector stood at the edge of the clearing, taking in the whole scene. It reminded him vaguely of the Wicked Uncles and the Babes in the Wood.

The private looked up: "Their heads have been bashed in, sir. Looks as if Grandiman got here first."

The major stood up a little sheepishly. "Wanted to see what they were really like," he explained, as if in self-defense.

"You shouldn't have disturbed them," said Manning severely, all his professional instincts coming to the fore.

"No need to look for clues, Manning. It's pretty obvious. They've only been gone a few minutes, I should say. Grandiman must have heard us coming, and sheered off."

"My men are working in, and yours are working out," the inspector said almost as if to himself. "So he should get caught between both parties—if it was only a *few* minutes ago."

He gazed pensively at the two fragile bodies. Inspector Manning did not regard himself as a highly imaginative man: he preferred to leave *that* kind of imagination to the intellectuals of the force. But as he stood there, a grim and vivid picture floated through his mind. He saw these two Romanesque, almost doll-like urchins wandering through this strange terrestrial forest. He saw the look of surprise on their faces when confronted with their first—and last—earthling; a look that must have changed to horror a moment later; a look that was now indelibly set upon their young, curiously innocent faces. He thought of their journey, of the silver machine coursing its silent, unknown miles through the hard and starry darkness to keep a fatal rendezvous.

The inspector stared down at the tiny twisted bodies—the fragile bodies of delicate children. And how the devil did people like this make and use a machine like that? he asked himself. But now he would never know—not till the next time.

A gust of wind brought a few remaining leaves down from the surrounding trees. Some of them fell, a symbolic terrestrial benediction, on the two inert forms. But these two childlike beings from another world were entirely oblivious of the color, the restless scent, the peculiar beauty of an English autumn.

The chill wind recalled Inspector Manning to his duties. "Let's go and get Grandiman before he gets up to any more tricks," he said tartly. "The blasted maniac has done enough damage for one morning. I bet they stick him back in the mental home and go all psychological on him!" he added bitterly.

"Won't there be a trial for murder?" asked the major.

The inspector glanced at the bodies again. *That* was a nice little problem!

His meditations were suddenly interrupted by a coarse, almost animal cry about a hundred yards away. Then there were sounds of many feet crashing through the forest. Then there was silence.

The major and the inspector gazed at the blank barrier of trees around them.

"Martin, stay here and look after these two until we come back," said the major.

"Yes, sir." The soldier's face was expressionless, but he was not amused. He noticed that the arm of one of the "children" seemed to be glowing slightly where it lay in the shadow.

"And if Grandiman turns up again," added the inspector, "you needn't be gentle. Make sure you 'bash' first, but not too hard."

"Yes, sir!" The soldier put some enthusiasm into his reply.

As they went vaguely in the direction of the noise, they heard footsteps coming their way. Inspector Manning put a finger over his lips, and stood still. The major did likewise. The other footsteps stopped. The major released the safety catch of his pistol, just in case.

Suddenly there were sounds of running feet, and Lieutenant Willow appeared. He had been tying his shoelace.

"Damn near got a bullet, Willow," said the major angrily, his hopes of a singlehanded—almost singlehanded—capture dashed to the ground.

"Sorry, sir," said Lieutenant Willow.

"You would have been," muttered the major darkly.

"Made any contact with Grandiman?" asked the inspector.

"Oh, him! Yes, we've collared him, sir. I was coming to tell you. He showed fight; I'm afraid he's a little damaged."

"Who got him?" asked Major Nore. "And who damaged him?"

"Sergeant West, sir, performed both operations."

"Good man!"

"I'll have to take charge of him," said the inspector formally.

Grandiman was taken back to the police van on the Falconford road. His face was badly bruised and his forehead was cut but he sat there quietly enough, though every now and then there was a loud crack as he dealt with the hazel nuts he had managed to pick up in Falcon Chase. Already the events of the morning were growing dim in his mind.

It was then that Sir Alan Leclerc, the chief constable, arrived. He gazed at the overturned police car and raised an eyebrow; he gazed at the unconscious signaler who had been removed from the oak; he gazed at the denuded trees, and at the strained faces of Inspector Manning and his companions.

Then Sir Alan said, "You'd better tell me the worst, Manning. I've heard rumours of secret weapons and heaven knows what!"

"The worst is, sir," said Inspector Manning dryly, "that we appear to have received a—a spaceship."

"One of ours, I trust," said Sir Alan, with a comfortable after-breakfast laugh.

But the inspector explained briefly, and then took him to see the remains. And after that Sir Alan Leclerc had neither the energy nor the inclination to laugh for many days.

The Prime Minister was informed before ten o'clock. He and the Home Secretary were on the spot before midday. By which time the story had leaked out and, as far as the county police were concerned, hell was let loose.

The newspapers had their fling; and it took a number of very soothing radio talks by a number of eminent men—including the P.M.—to persuade the world in general, and Britain in particular, that they were not yet in danger of planetary invasion. Nobody was really convinced—least of all the Prime Minister.

But, unbelievably, after the first hectic excitement it all began to drift into dream dimensions. Presently the headlines grew smaller; the doom prophets simmered down; conversation in the morning trains imperceptibly returned to normal; and the earth continued to revolve placidly along its orbit around the sun.

Because nothing else happened. And finally there grew the comfortable feeling that nothing else would happen. . . . Until the next time.

The single oil lamp in the Best Room of The Green Man appeared to Sir Alan Leclerc, after three large brandies, to be a kind of symbol: sanity in a world of drifting shadows.

"It *wasn't* a dream, damn it!" he said indignantly.

"It was not," agreed Inspector Mannig, gazing at the dark

liquid in his tankard. "I'll tell you what, sir. It seemed as if we were all a lot of characters that had walked into the first act of a play we didn't know."

Inspector Manning, the man who prided himself upon his lack of imagination, had hit the nail on the head. He had expressed not only the feelings of those who had taken part in the brief drama of Falcon Chase, but also the mood of alert bewilderment that had briefly gripped a waiting world.

Major Nore broke the brief silence that followed the Inspector's odd remark. "I wonder what the next act will be, and when it will happen."

Sir Alan gazed into the fire. "Tomorrow, Major. Or the day after. Or the next century, or the century after that. After all, what do we know of *their* time?"

The inspector looked at the chief constable. "Talking of *them*, sir, what did you make of the bodies?"

Sir Alan said slowly: "Somehow, Manning, when I looked at their childlike faces and those—there's only one word for it—those *innocent* eyes, I was reminded of Genesis."

"Don't see the connection, I'm afraid." The major felt it was all becoming a little metaphysical.

"Work it out, Major." The chief constable turned to the inspector again. "By the way, Manning, I had a little talk with Professor Ryles this afternoon. He's willing to stake his reputation that they were at least four hundred years old!"

The inspector digested this information for a moment or two. Then he recalled a vivid picture of autumn leaves falling upon the Babes in the Wood.

"Yes, sir. But not four hundred of *our* years," said Inspector Manning, displaying a wisdom greater than he would ever realize.

THE JAR OF LATAKIA

Mallory lifted the makeshift lid of the tankard and sniffed curiously. It was just an ordinary stoneware tankard, the kind one used to buy full of mustard in pre-war Vienna. There was a crude, dark red bas--relief of St. Nikolaus on the side.

But the tankard did not now contain mustard. A few stiff, dried flakes of what appeared to be tobacco lay at the bottom. It smelled like tobacco and it felt like tobacco—the kind of tobacco that might have been mislaid round about the turn of the century. There seemed to be a little less than half an ounce.

A confirmed pipe-smoker and *soi-disant* connoisseur of tobacco, Mallory fingered the brittle flakes and held them lose to his nose for a new moments.

"Latakia," he pronounced audibly and confidently, feeling sure of his verdict.

At that point there was a knock at the door. Mallory put the Latakia back into the tankard, which he returned to the oven of the disused kitchen range, where he had found it. Then he went to receive his visitor, and promptly forgot all about it.

John Mallory had occupied the country cottage for about a month. The fact that the previous owner, a Colonel Harrys, had hanged himself upon a convenient apple tree in the garden made the purchase of the cottage an easy matter. Mallory had offered a ridiculously low sum which had promptly been accepted.

For Mallory, the attraction of Rone House lay in its isolation. He wanted to get on with his work, and for that he needed solitude. City life might have its merits and consolations for the struggling artist; but for the successful one, as Mallory had found to his cost, it also had its limitations. One was expected to entertain and be entertained. One was expected to scintillate in a miasma of rather vapid parties. One was expected to be gregarious and eccentric, and to use a studio largely for the cultivation of multiple and complex love affairs.

In such a world John Mallory was out of character. Thirty-five years old and a bachelor with a reasonable income, he felt just a little vulnerable. And of late his vulnerability had been tested by one or two aspiring women, single and otherwise. From these and from other distractions he had fled into the country. Now, at last, he was beginning to get down to solid work again.

The north bedroom of the cottage made a comfortable studio. Mallory did not regret the loss of rustling silk or taffeta and the bright red smiles. At Rone House he met only those human beings it was necessary to meet—chiefly tradespeople. He lived alone and liked it.

One morning shortly after breakfast he took himself up to the studio to continue work on a rather ambitious portrait. It was the head and shoulders of a woman—the kind of woman John Mallory had never known. He needed no model, and was guided only by the fleeting but profound impressions that his waking mind managed to retain from a persistent though damnably elusive dream.

On this particular morning he was engaged in the delicate project of painting the eyes. Three times he had scraped the paint off the canvas with his palette knife. The light was good, his working conditions were excellent, but somehow the colors were muddy. Mallory gazed at his untidy palette with distaste. None of the pigments upon it possessed the quality he needed. The blues were dull and lifeless; the greens stodgy and opaque. How then could he hope to achieve the transparent and luminous turquoise that would bring those vacant eyes to a mysterious, independent life?

He puffed furiously at his pipe, concentrating upon the insoluble problem. Presently he noticed that the pipe was cold. Muttering an irritable curse, he reached for his pouch, recalling as he did so that he had taken the last filling after breakfast. Mallory cursed freely and stalked grimly downstairs in vain but hopeful search for an odd tin of tobacco.

After five minutes he gave it up and bestowed eloquent if unreasonable maledictions on the village shop that was nearly two miles away.

It was then that Mallory remembered the jar of Latakia. He went into the kitchen and took it from the old kitchen range. Removing the lid, he stared at the dark, crisp shreds distastefully.

"Poisonous stuff!" he muttered to himself. But at that particular point Mallory was prepared to burn his throat out, if only he was allowed to solve the problem of the eyes.

So he decided to brew a mug of tea as an antidote to the probable effects of smoking that dry and ancient tobacco. Waiting for the kettle to boil, he idly mused upon this first and only relic of Colonel Harrys that remained in the cottage. He began to wonder why the colonel—from all accounts a stock military type—should choose such a dramatic way of taking his life.

"Probably smoked too much of this damn tobacco," he concluded uncharitably. Then, as steam came from the spout of the kettle, he considered the possibility that the Latakia might have been in Rone House long before Colonel Harrys came.

Back in the studio, Mallory banished all such conjectures from his mind as he contemplated the canvas before him, occasionally sipping tea, and absently stuffing shreds of Latakia into his pipe.

Presently the fragrance peculiar to such tobacco began to

fill the studio, blue skeins of smoke wreathing leisurely across the still atmosphere.

Presently Mallory found a more promising way of approaching his problem; and then, naturally, simply, inevitably, the means of solving it. He began to work quickly and silently.

Presently, a pair of blue-green, slightly luminous eyes regarded him gravely from the enigmatic canvas.

The girl was sitting in the chair when Mallory awoke. She was staring at him gravely with the same blue-green eyes.

His heart lurched violently and he glanced with a terrible effort of will at the canvas. Nothing had changed. Here, then, was the original of the painting.

Mallory sat up suddenly on his campbed and gaped. The reality of the situation began to penetrate the sleepy mist that still shrouded his returning consciousness. More important than solving the mystery of how he came to be asleep on the campbed was this urgent, three-dimensional mystery of the girl.

"In God's name, who are you?" demanded Mallory, his voice sharp with a peculiar fear. He heard his own taut words break the silence, and was startled by their intensity.

The unreasonable surge of fear drowned all rational feeling, swept away all common-sense explanations or possibilities, as Mallory took in the details of her odd dress: the long divided skirt gleaming like dull metal; the black translucent spiderweb of blouse, offset by curious brooches; the broad belt around her waist. And even as the scene burned itself indelibly into his mind, he registered the insignificant fact that the clock had stopped—at twenty past eleven. Therefore he had been asleep for less than five minutes, or more than twenty-four hours.

From the sluggish stupidity of awakening, his thoughts had accelerated to a breakneck speed, so that his mind was busy exploring all possibilities before the girl had answered his question.

Her voice, leisurely and musical, was like a cool sedative to Mallory's high fever of unreason.

"It is natural for you to be afraid," she said. "That is why I wanted you to awaken slowly—to lessen the shock. . . . Please look into my eyes!"

It was neither a request nor a command, yet Mallory instantly acceded or obeyed; he was not sure which.

For a moment the deep luminosity of her gaze seemed to darken the room, seemed to swallow him; and he felt drawn through opaque, swirling pools of darkness. Then everything was light again. But he no longer felt tense or afraid. Calmly and intelligently he awaited her explanation.

She smiled. "That feels better, doesn't it?"

He nodded. "Who are you?" he asked once again. But the terror had left his voice.

"First let me prepare you," she said in the odd, leisurely tone. "It would be better, I think, if you could accept this experience as a rather vivid dream—nothing more. You see, your mind is not attuned to face this particular actuality without suffering a great stress. Can you believe that you are dreaming?"

Once more he met the compelling darkness of her eyes.

"If you think it is necessary," he said calmly, "I will believe that I am dreaming." He turned toward the canvas. "But, as you see, the dream has not entirely taken me by surprise."

She followed his glance and her smile became almost mischievous. "Naturally there would be a certain amount of subsconscious preparation," she explained. "Your—your submerged self would anticipate this experience long before your conscious self was able to enter it."

Mallory, already accepting the dreamlike quality of the situation, was beginning to react almost naturally. "I'm not sure that I believe in predestination," he remarked with a thinly disguised skepticism. "Or even in clairvoyance."

She seemed to be amused. "You won't deny that there is a certain relation between cause and effect?"

Her amusement was infectious. After all, thought Mallory, if this is a dream, then I'll have a damn good two cents' worth. And if it isn't a dream, it's certainly diverting.

He shook his head in answer to her question. "Nevertheless I do assert that there is such a thing as free will."

As if by chance, her gaze rested on Mallory's pipe, which lay on the floor. He noticed it—and remembered the Latakia —for the first time.

"Did that have anything to do with it?" he asked quickly.

The girl's eyes were laughing. "Perhaps," she said noncommittally.

Mallory felt he was making a fool of himself.

Then suddenly she became serious. "The first thing you must accept," she said, "is that we exist in different kinds of time." She paused to let the full meaning of her words sink in.

There was a few seconds' silence, during which Mallory became unaccountably cold. He stared at her, trying to comprehend the strange transition from a normal studio session to a tightrope walk between daydream and nightmare.

"You mean," he said hoarsely, "you belong to the past?"

For a moment the girl looked surprised. Then the latent power in her eyes seemed to reach out and hold him.

"No, Mr. Mallory," she said quietly. "But I'm afraid you do!" He began to smile again. "You see," she added gently, yet with a curious compulsion, "I happen to know that you died nearly a hundred years ago!"

Looking out of the window, Mallory knew beyond doubt that what she had said was true.

Until twenty-past eleven—or, more accurately, until he had fallen asleep—the view from the studio window had been a panorama of woodland. This was now replaced by the runway of a vast airfield; and in the distance was a cluster of strange, shiny hemispheres which—so the girl told him—were hangars. Mallory was inclined to believe her—especially as a huge aircraft, a slender wingless fuselage, had just passed overhead with terrifying silence.

There were beads of moisture on his forehead, but his hands were ominously cold. It became vitally necessary to keep on talking: a pathetic attempt to assert his own existence. The girl standing by his side watched him with a curious, intimate detachment.

"But this is all nonsense!" he exploded. "It just isn't so! It's some kind of delusion. I—I—"

"It is so," she asserted simply, with a hint of compassion in her voice. "But for you, I agree, it is nonsense. It is outside your terms of reference—just as your own world is beyond my experience."

"Look here," said Mallory harshly, "how the devil do you fit into this bloody nightmare?"

The girl studied his tense expression, trying to will him into a calmer state of mind. "I've already told you," she said patiently. "I am what you would call, I think, a psychiatric worker. It is my business to study certain peculiar experiences which, in your day, were supposed to be simple hallucinations."

"And I," said Mallory sardonically, "am therefore one of your guinea pigs."

"Exactly. We have reason to believe that Time, or History, or Experience—call it what you will—is playing some rather strange tricks in this cottage. I am, so to speak, investigating the reputed hauntings." She smiled suddenly. "May I say that I find you a very interesting and human sort of ghost?"

Mallory was not deceived by the lightness of her tone. "There have been others?" he asked quickly.

She nodded. "One, at least. Perhaps more. You see, we were able to localize the disturbances only shortly before the appearance of our last visitor."

Mallory took a leap in the dark: "Colonel Harrys?"

"Did you know him?" countered the girl quickly.

Mallory gave a bitter laugh. "He hanged himself. That's how I came to get the cottage."

"We know all about his death," she said. "Poor man, he was unable to stand the shock. You, on the other hand, are taking it much better."

"Which just goes to show that psychiatry hasn't advanced a great deal," he remarked dryly.

Possibly not. But telepathy has. You must remember, Mr. Mallory, that unless you choose to shut me out, I can witness most of your thoughts."

Mallory stared at her. Then a slight smile played about his lips.

"It's no use trying to shock me," she said imperturbably. "It is perfectly natural of you to think of me as a woman and to use your imagination to satisfy your curiosity. . . . I accept the compliment in the spirit in which it is given."

He detected a slight glitter in her eyes and was suddenly pleased. "People must be pretty uninhibited in this brave new world," he remarked with a thin smile.

"They need to be," said the girl evenly.

The clock was still at eleven-twenty; the portrait was still on the easel; the airfield was still visible through the window; and the girl had not yet disappeared.

Mallory had recovered himself sufficiently to offer some tea to her—the pot he had brewed was still extraordinarily hot—and he went down to the kitchen for an extra cup and saucer. There he discovered the kettle still puffing steam through its spout, though he remembered turning the gas out before, as he noted grimly, he had turned into a ghost. He began to have his own idea of the kind of dimension in which he now found himself.

On his return to the studio, he watched the girl sip her cup of tea with intense curiosity. He was disappointed. Nothing happened.

"Tell me," he said suddenly, "did I fall, or was I pushed?"

The girl regarded him thoughtfully. "I imagine you pushed yourself, Mr. Mallory. We—of the present time, or your future—certainly had no hand in it, if that is what you think."

Mallory was silent for a moment or two. Then he said, "I expect Colonel Harrys was a pipe-smoker, too."

The girl chose to appear puzzled. "Does that have any bearing?" Then she added, "I see you are thinking about some peculiar tobacco you have smoked."

Mallory laughed. "A jar of Latakia. A few harmless shreds of Latakia. A Viennese mustard pot stuffed away idly in an old kitchen range. . . . You people of the future seem to be good at riddles—what do you make of that?"

"You want me to say that it has strange properties," she answered quietly. "That, in fact, it is responsible for projecting you a hundred years forward. But I don't know—and neither, I think, do you."

"Oh, yes, *I* do," said Mallory. "I know damn well! But it's good to find that the inhabitants of this brave new world are not omniscient, after all. There are more things, Horatio, than are dreamt of in your telepathy." He began to laugh at his own misquotation. He began to laugh raucously and loudly.

She slapped his face. The laughter stopped suddenly. Mallory stared vacantly through the window. "Thank you," he said in an unsteady voice. "I'm sorry."

"You began your painting before you touched this Latakia," she said abruptly. "How did you come to paint my portrait?"

"It came in a dream," said Mallory in a toneless murmur. "It came in a dream, and I was haunted by the eyes of someone I would never know. Now, I have met you, and it is different. Because one cannot love the future: one can only be afraid, damnably afraid. Or mad. . . . When did I die?"

For a moment the girl was off guard. His sudden glance caught the brief pity in her eyes.

"At the end of your life," she replied softly. "And that is when each of us dies, at the end of his life."

"The year," insisted Mallory. "What year? You said you knew!"

"I do know, but it is not good that I should tell you. Besides, I do not know the year in which you left your own world."

"Nineteen fifty-six," he said quickly. "What year did I die?"

The girl did not meet his gaze. For the first time she seemed unsure of herself. "Nineteen eighty-eight," she said hesitantly. "I am as foolish to tell you as you are to ask."

"Liar," said Mallory cheerfully. "It's comforting to know

that women haven't learned to lie any better. You might have fooled Harrys, but not me. I have painted your eyes."

"And what did you see there?"

"The truth!"

"What is the truth?"

"Ask Jesting Pilate," taunted Mallory.

"It is time you went back," she said quickly.

Mallory pointed to the clock. "I have abolished time. Time will stand still until I'm ready for it."

"It is dangerous to stay."

"I accept the danger," he said recklessly. "I have conquered time to find my ideal woman, and now I am told to go back. Your attitude, my dear, is essentially feminine. You should never have tempted a homeless ghost."

His vision was becoming blurred, but he could still see her eyes. They spoke to him silently from a great distance. In them he recognized the truth of his own careless words. But already it was too late.

"What is your name?" he demanded, standing still and swaying like a drunken man. "Whose name shall I call when the stars are dark? Whose portrait shall I gaze at in this empty room?"

Now the room itself was fading. He could no longer see her. Yet when she spoke her voice was low and close.

"I am Ann," she whispered, "and you are John. Don't you see, we can't be ourselves because we are separated by time! You must go back! You must enter your own world again."

"Ann, where are you? I can't see any more! Give me your hand!"

She gave him her hand, hoping to lead him to the camp bed and force him to relax. But with a sudden, surprising vigor, Mallory took her in his arms, blindly seeking her lips.

The darkness became a whirlpool, and slowly the whirlpool grew into a sea of silence.

The hammer crashed again and again, relentlessly. Mallory opened his eyes slowly, very slowly. He looked toward the sound of the hammer. The clock fingers pointed to twenty past eleven. The hammer blows subsided into a steady, even ticking.

Mallory looked about him in bewilderment and fear, half expecting the room, with all its maddening stillness, to dissolve into yet another timeless dream. But the room remained, quiet and eloquent, mute with secrets. The only evidence of that strange interlude was the extra cup and saucer, lying by the chair.

The cup was still warm—still bearing the imprint, thought Mallory bitterly, of those elusive lips.

He heard an echo of that voice—the soft, low voice that was a hundred years away: *I am Ann, and you are John. Don't you see, we can't be ourselves because we are separated by time! You must go back. . . .*

"Blast it, I've come back!" he shouted hopelessly. "Back to a quiet dose of madness!"

Suddenly his gaze fell on the canvas. The blue-green, slightly luminous eyes met his own in a level, vacant stare. The lips were immobile, silent; and he knew that he would never hear them speak again—unless . . .

"Hell and damnation!" he sobbed, fighting the urge to shake and crush the canvas in an insane effort to force it into becoming the living woman.

Mallory fled from the room, afraid of doing violence to all that was left of his dream.

Down in the kitchen, his trembling fingers held the jar of Latakia. There were, perhaps, three fillings left. His first impulsive was to hurl the jar and its contents through the window; his second impulse was to preserve it carefully, against the time when he would recover the necessary courage to re-create, in his studio, the conditions for—madness.

Mallory shuddered, and replaced the tobacco in its accustomed hiding place. There were beads of moisture on his forehead; for he knew now that his will was broken, and knew also that he could never enter that room again.

Two days later, haggard, unshaven, sleepless, he came to what appeared to be the only reasonable decision. Having made it, Mallory felt curiously free.

There remained but one or two letters to write. When they were finished he went briskly about the task of hunting up a piece of old rubber piping he remembered having see somewhere. Having found it he made his way to the garage. He smiled grimly to himself, knowing that Colonel Harrys, at least, would have understood.

Later, the coroner and other interested persons would doubtless dwell upon the unusual phenomenon of a man committing suicide while calmly smoking his pipe.

Rone House had been empty and quiet for some time; its reputation was not forgotten and the executors were unable to sell it even at a ridiculously nominal price.

Prospective buyers would suspiciously inspect the attractive country cottage, testing every beam and floor-board seeking some explanation for the tempting sum at which it was offered. The vendors naturally were vague and reticent. But the occasional prospective tenants would uncover a detailed and startling history (factual and otherwise) over a leisurely tankard at any of the nearby village taverns. Thereafter, as they were warned in slow country dialect, they pursued the matter at their own risk. It was eighteen months before anyone did so.

He was a young man in his early thirties, an impecunious novelist in search of solitude and atmosphere. A pleasant, intelligent young man, skeptical and credulous.

He picked his way up the grassy drive one fine spring morning with the agent's keys in his hands. In sunlight, Rone House looked an attractive proposition. The interior had been throughly cleaned and decorated. Even the old kitchen range seemed bright and serviceable.

The young man was not yet to know that in the disused oven there lay a stoneware tankard containing a few dark, brittle shreds. He surveyed the cottage with satisfaction, impulsively deciding that there, if anywhere, was the place to finish his book.

It was a fine warm day, and the spring optimism was infectious. Oddly enough, the new tenant was a confirmed pipe smoker.

M 81: URSA MAJOR

> Motion does not tire anybody. With the earth as our vehicle we are traveling at 20 miles a second around the sun; the sun carries us at 12 miles a second through the galactic system; the galactic system bears us at 250 miles a second amid the spiral nebulae; the spiral nebulae . . . If motion could tire, we ought to be dead tired. *Sir Arthur Eddington,*
> THE NATURE OF THE PHYSICAL WORLD

It was twenty hours, ship's time, after firing point. A million miles astern, Earth shone coldly like a small green moon. On the navigation deck of the *Santa Maria,* a profound silence was disturbed only by the steady but discreet ping of the radio probe.

Captain Mauris leaned back on his contour-berth and

waited patiently for his soul to catch up with his body. His sensations at the beginning of each deep voyage were invariably the same. His body had learned to adapt to a force of 10 G and to a stellar acceleration whose graph was a mad ascending curve; but his spirit, while hardly weak, retained the old subconscious reluctance. It didn't much care for the big jump. It would hang tenaciously onto the illusion that Captain Mauris would presently wake up to find himself at home in bed.

He rarely did, because, more often than not, the dream became the reality. Recently he had calculated that he had slept on Earth not more than nine thousand times in his life, whereas he had voyaged among the stars for nearly twice that number of Earth nights. It was the sort of calculation that he did not care to remember—which was principally why he could not forget it.

Which was the dream—Earth or space? After twenty hours of space flight in planetary drive (which nowadays the younger men humorously called first gear) Captain Mauris was not too sure of the answer. He had long ago ceased to have physical space-sickness, but he had never lost the spiritual variety. And lately it had seemed to intensify. Perhaps he was just getting old. Perhaps he really would make this the last trip. . . .

The captain sighed, and took refuge in the monumental assumption of Descartes: *I think; therefore I exist.* He began to wonder whether the same could be said of his boatload of physicists. With a sardonic smile Captain Mauris decided that he had seen terrestrial positronic robots that could lay a greater claim to individuality.

Ever since the dim, distant days of the twentieth century, when the scientific caste system had been formalized, physicists had tended to become less and less human, and now they were hardly more than semi-substantial extrapolations of their own theories.

They were a race apart. Watching them board the *Santa Maria*, listening to their conversation, Captain Mauris had actually wondered whether they might be the new type of omega robots which, according to rumor, were now past the experimental stage. But he had seen two of them playing chess so badly, and a third so delightfully green with space-sickness, that he had regretfully concluded that they were human. Even *sigma* robots played chess excellently, and clearly there was no reason why the robot engineers should endow their offspring with uncontrollable nervous systems. The physicists, then, were unfortunately human—a sad comment on the sort of civilization that allowed robots to take charge of global production, while turning the best human brains into second-rate electronic calculators.

The captain's private soliloquy was interrupted by Phylo, the first officer, climbing down from the astrodome.

"Dead on," said Phylo. "Heading straight for *Zeta* of the Great Bear. When do we change gear, Captain?"

Captain Mauris gave him a sour look. "While I command the *Santa Maria*, Mr. Phylo, we will not change gear."

"Sorry, sir. When do we use the stellar drive, then?"

"I think," replied the captain, "that I will shortly inquire if the physicists are still alive and, if so, when they will be prepared to take the bump."

Phylo laughed. "I hope you're disappointed, sir."

"Meaning what?"

"I hope they're still kicking. I should hate to have to return to earth and explain why we knocked off six top S.F.P.'S."

"The world," said Captain Mauris soberly, "might smell somewhat sweeter for the loss of a few space-frame physicists. Man is becoming just a little too clever."

"I wonder why you volunteered for the trip, then," said Phylo slyly. "A voyage with S.F.P. men for unspecified experimental purposes hardly promises to be uneventful. Besides, there's the triple danger money—just like the old days when they first tried out the stellar drive."

"Of the few parts of the world that remain unspoiled by civilization, the Amazonian hinterland is the most attractive —for me," said Captain Mauris obliquely. "One of these days, Phylo, I shall buy myself ten thousand acres in the middle of nowhere. And then the only time I shall ever take my feet off terra firma will be when I climb into my hammock. The reason I signed on as master of the *Santa Maria* is quite simple. It represents almost five thousand acres."

"If," said Phylo dryly, "we survive whatever tricks the S.F.P.'s are cooking up."

"Exactly," said Captain Mauris. "But it is my firm intention to survive."

Phylo gazed through the plastiglass anti-glare dome at a swarm of hard, unwinking suns. Finally, without looking at Mauris, he said softly, "I think there's also another reason, sir."

"Do you, now!" The captain's tone was not encouraging. Phylo took a deep breath and plowed on. "They told me back at base that you were the first skipper to successfully use the stellar drive."

"A slight exaggeration," said Mauris with a cold smile. "I was merely the first captain to return and collect his pay envelope. However, proceed."

"I notice," said Phylo uneasily, "that there's a parallel set of gears—I mean dual controls—on the main panel."

"Well?"

"I don't understand the calibrations on the dials under the lightometer. Nor do I understand why the second bank of meters should have all their throw-in switches locked and sealed."

"An interesting little mystery," observed the captain noncommittally. "As you have obviously given some thought to it, what conclusion do you draw?"

"Well, sir," said Phylo hesitantly, "bearing in mind that the *Santa Maria* has a cargo of S.F.P.'s, a skipper who successfully tested the stellar drive, a set of new instruments, and the fact that we are under sealed orders, I think there's only one possible conclusion."

"I should be interested to hear it," said Captain Mauris.

"There have been rumors," continued Phylo, "of a galactic drive. My guess is that the *Santa Maria* has been fitted out for a trial run. What do you think, sir?"

"I think," replied Captain Mauris, glancing at the bulkhead electrochron, "that I shall shortly break the seal and discover what the Fates have in store for us. I'll tell you this, though: I don't think we shall be experimenting with a galactic drive."

"Why not, sir?"

"Because," said Captain Mauris with a thin smile, "the United Space Corporation has already developed it—as a logical extension of the steller drive."

Phylo gazed at him in sheer amazement. "It's the first I've heard of it, sir."

"I know," said Mauris imperturbably. "It's still on the secret list. But since I traveled as a paid observer on the test jump I can definitely assure you that the galactic drive is a fact."

Phylo's voice was filled with awe. "Would it be indiscreet to inquire what distance you logged?"

"Not now," said the captain. "I think—in view of our position—that it will do no harm to give you the facts. We—er—had a little jaunt round Beta Centauri."

"Godalmighty!"

"A matter of seven hundred light-years for the round trip," added Mauris complacently.

"How long did it take?" demanded Phylo incredulously.

The captain permitted a note of pride to enter his voice. "Three hours, twenty-seven minutes, ship's time—starting and finishing in the neighborhood of Pluto's orbit."

"Were there any—any casualties?"

"All of us," said Captain Mauris soberly. "We couldn't stop laughing for two days. But I forgot. There was one serious casualty: Egon, the navigator. His star-maps were damn near useless, of course. He swore we'd never get home. And when we finally hit the System, the relief was too much for him. He was the only one who didn't stop laughing. And from what I hear he's still enjoying himself."

Phylo couldn't make up his mind whether or not Captain Mauris was having a private joke. After a moment or two, he said in a matter-of-fact voice, "I wonder what the hell is going to happen on this trip, then?"

"Probably," said Captain Mauris, "we shall cease to exist."

Four hours later in the privacy of his cabin the captain of the *Santa Maria* broke the seal on a slim envelope and read his instructions. He skipped impatiently through the conventional wording until he came to the part that mattered. He went through it carefully, word for word, three times. The final paragraph gave him a certain grim amusement.

While the normal articles of space travel obtain for this experimental voyage, he read, *there must of necessity be a fluid definition of the safety clause. Clearly the primary responsibility of the master for the safety of his ship and all personnel must be to some extent subordinated to the actual program sanctioned by the Field Testing Executive of the United Space Corporation. It is not implied, however, that the prerogative of master's discretion will inevitably be superseded by test requirements. If the master should satisfy himself, and the authorized scientists concerned, that the danger factor is sufficient to render the ship's safe return improbable, therefore neutralizing the validity of the experiment, he is entitled to cancel the test program and return immediately to base. A court of inquiry will then evaluate the circumstances leading to such a decision. It is, however, earnestly hoped that scientific and ship personnel will so co-operate as to bring both the experiment and the voyage to a successful conclusion.*

"Why the devil," said Captain Mauris to himself, "do they

use a lot of big words to tell me that I'm merely acting wet nurse for a bunch of S.F.P.'s? *If the master should satisfy himself, and the authorized scientists concerned . . .* Very funny! The whole idea is not less than one hundred per cent suicidal, and they talk about a sufficient danger factor!"

There was a knock at the door.

"Come in," called Mauris.

It was Kobler, chief of the S.F.P. team. He was a thin, pasty-faced man of perhaps forty. His mouth looked as if it would split if he tried to smile.

Mauris motioned him into a chair and reached for two glasses and the decanter. As Mauris poured the drinks Kobler glanced at the ship's articles lying on the desk.

"I see you have been studying the scriptures," said the physicist.

"I was merely trying to find out," explained Captain Mauris equably, "what authority, if any, I possess—in case of an emergency."

"And have you found out?" inquired Kobler, sipping his whisky.

"Yes."

"Are you satisfied?"

"No. From the point of view of getting a clear-cut definition, it's as woolly as hell."

"I shouldn't worry, if I were you," said Kobler pleasantly. "If anything goes wrong you'll probably have a minisecond in which to think a last beautiful thought."

"That," retorted Mauris thinly, "is why I would have liked sufficient power to overrule you people—just in case I happened to anticipate the hypothetically fatal minisecond."

"Sorry," said Kobler, "but I'm the boss-man. That's the way it has to be for this sort of thing. You'd better resign yourself to praying for my spiritual guidance."

"I don't know why you people need a space captain," said Mauris testily. "You could have programed the *Santa Maria* to take you to dissolution point under her own steam."

Kobler smiled, and his face didn't crack. "You may not believe it," he said ironically, "but we space-frame gentry have nice orderly minds. We're very conventional really. Besides, even a space captain has his uses. . . . How did you enjoy the hop round Beta Centauri?"

"So that was why they wanted me to go," said Mauris. "I wondered about it."

"You were lucky," said Kobler. "They wouldn't let me go because some idiot mathematician suggested that the ship might surface too near a sun, or something damn silly like that. It seems that my brain was considered too valuable to be fried."

"Mine evidently wasn't," observed the captain.

"You, my friend, are unique," said Kobler dryly. "You are a veteran of the stellar drive and the galactic jump. We regard you as a curio, a kind of talisman."

"I am flattered," said Captain Mauris. "And now, I think, we had better discuss ways and means."

"You know the destination?" asked Kobler.

The captain inclined his head toward the papers on the desk. "According to the Field Testing Executive," he said calmly, "it is Messier 81."

"What do you think of it?" asked Kobler smugly.

"I think it might be—interesting," said Captain Mauris with sarcasm. "I don't think I've ever visited a spiral nebula before."

Kobler grinned. "One million six hundred thousand light-years," he said. "Quite a little hop when you come to think of it."

"How long do you think it will take?"

The physicist's grin broadened. "I don't know," he said happily. "Probably just that hypothetically fatal minisecond."

Mauris restrained himself with an effort. "I'd appreciate a brief exposition of the theory," he said. "It might be useful."

Kobler helped himself to more whisky, leaned back in his chair and regarded the ceiling. "Essentially," he began, "it involves my private theory of matter, which also involves the stress characteristic of space and the so-called temporal regression."

"Proceed," said Mauris. "For a moment I thought you were going to get complicated."

Kobler ignored him. "You understand, of course," he continued, "that matter is a form of locked-up energy?"

"Yes."

"Good. I now have news for you. Energy is simply a form of locked-up space. There is, from the physicist's point of view, quite a reasonable amount of energy in the cosmos; there is also the devil of a lot of space. Now there is, as well, the curious phenomenon of the expansion and unwrinkling of space alongside the actual diminution of energy."

"You wouldn't be throwing overboard the first and second laws of thermodynamics, would you?" interrupted the captain mildly.

Kobler admired his own fingernails complacently.

"Child's play," he said. "Entropy and the first and second laws are all washed up. Funny thing, when I was a student I instinctively knew there was something wrong. But back to the point. I have established a definite coefficient, the practical application of which means, my friend, that we too can adopt the charming habit of energy. We can *submerge* in space. Just as energy, when it thinks nobody is looking, opens a little door into the fifth dimension and smartly sidesteps all detection by *becoming* space, so we can play the same trick. Only we can go one better: we can become energy again. Which, in effect, means that we can knock the mainspring out of time. Because, Captain Mauris, by becoming virtually nonexistent we escape the temporal regression. That, in a simpler fashion, is why you were able to hop round Beta Centauri and swallow seven hundred light-years. And of the three hours twenty-seven minutes it took, you spent most of the time surfacing so that Egon could panic over his star-maps."

"That is true," said Mauris. "But—if you will forgive a simple space captain for pointing out the obvious—we were functioning in a known energy system. By making the new target M 81, you are postulating a jump clean out of the local energy pattern."

"Not *out* of, but *through*," corrected the physicist. "On the Beta Centauri trip you were still slightly limited by a temporal regression. This time the deceleration will be so sharp as to make a total breakthrough. We shall make a neat hole in our own space frame and enter sub-space. We shall become a pattern of space on the frame of sub-space. Then we shall localize our return breakthrough when a pretty little instrument that I have programed for M 81 recognizes the surface energy pattern."

"Suppose the programing fails?"

Kobler laughed. "As it is the first true cosmometer, there is the possibility. But you can take it from me that it is theoretically perfect."

Captain Mauris though nostalgically of the Amazonian hinterland. After nearly a minute's silence he said, "It's nice to feel that somebody's confident, anyway."

"Space has a very definite direction," pursued Kobler. "Its vortices are the galactic leaks. In some respects we can regard the sub-echoes of nebulae as stepping stones. In the extragalactic jump it's chiefly a question of defining the direction/deceleration crisis—or, in plain language, of making the right hole at the right time."

"I expect you'll want to clear the System before the—er—experiment begins," ventured Mauris.

"Naturally," said Kobler. "By the way, would you like me to tell the crew what it's all about?"

"I was going to suggest a brief lecture," replied Mauris. "But since you have explained the background to me so lucidly, I think I might save you that little job. I'll tell them we're going to make a nice little hole in the balloon of space and pop up again sixteen hundred thousand light-years away. That should make for some interesting discussion."

"You think they'll panic?"

The captain shook his head. "They'll just laugh politely and think I'm getting too old for the job."

"So far as I can see," said Kobler, downing the remainder of his whisky, "everything is predictable—except the human reaction."

"It makes for a nice philosophical problem," observed Mauris.

"What does?"

"Whether or not we can be conscious of our own non-existence."

Kobler gave him a look of respect. "That's the crux of the matter," he admitted. "You see, the *Santa Maria* and all aboard will cease to be a system of molecular organizations."

"Conversely," said the captain in a matter-of-fact voice, "it will become the abstract memory of an energy pattern which will be resynthesized out of space—when and if your infallible cosmometer correlates the pattern of M 81 with that of its own environment."

Kobler sat up. "I didn't know you were a physicist."

"I'm not," retorted Mauris dryly. "But I'll tell you something else, too. It's going to be damn cold!"

Pluto's orbit was a hundred million miles astern, and the *Santa Maria* had achieved a satisfactory clearance of the System. For the last ten hours she had voyaged under her stellar drive. Through the dark plastiglass port holes men occasionally stared at the long star-torn silence of total night.

The navigation deck was a scene of activity and tension, for deceleration point was rapidly approaching. A fat copper cylinder had been battened to the deck in front of the main control panel, and the second bank of switches, with their mysterious calibrations, had now been unsealed. Kobler had lovingly supervised the installation of his cosmometer, and was now displaying sufficient humanity to fuss about it much

103

as an anxious father nursing his first-born. Phylo, the first officer, was surreptitiously biting his nails. He was definitely unhappy. His appreciation of the science of physics being rather more limited than usual for one in his position, he had come to believe simply that the approaching experiment was merely the most elaborate method yet invented of committing suicide.

Of all the personnel of the *Santa Maria*, Captain Mauris was the most calm. He was very busy breaking several regulations. He lay on his master's contour-berth and watched all the extra berths that were needed by the physicists being bolted down. Kobler had decided, after much consultation, that the entire S.F.P. team should foregather on the navigation deck for the experiment. Half a dozen extra berths had then been hastily erected, giving the impression of a surrealist hospital.

Normally Captain Mauris would have regarded the invasion with frigid resentment. But now he watched the proceedings with a benevolent air.

It was his duty as master of the ship to present at all times an aspect of confidence. With the aid of a bottle of Scotch and a somewhat prehistoric corncob pipe he was fulfilling this obligation admirably. He was also sweating, for he had discarded his uniform jacket in favor of two old polo-necked jerseys. Doubtless the Field Testing Executive would strongly disapprove of his unconventional approach, but then the F.T.E. were millions of miles away.

Having taken what he considered to be a sufficiency of spirit the captain was now engaged in chewing glucose tablets. Phylo watched him with silent awe.

Eventually Kobler looked up from his cosmometer. "Nine minutes to go, Captain," he said formally.

Mauris glanced at the bulkhead electrochron and nodded. "Five hundred seconds," he said pleasantly, "and then sixteen hundred thousand light-years. Science is quite wonderful."

Kobler was nettled. "What are you eating—nerve pills?"

"Glucose," said Mauris affably. "I've been dieting on whisky and glucose."

"Why?"

"Because," explained Mauris, "I intend to keep both warm and energetic."

"There should not be any drop in temperature," said Kobler. "In any case, the thermostat will fix it."

"The nonexistent thermostat," corrected Mauris gently.

"But I was not thinking of coldness that can be measured in degrees centigrade."

"There is no other," said Kobler authoritatively. "Neither is there any need to keep your strength up. There will be no fatigue."

"Nor was I thinking of physical fatigue."

Kobler shrugged. "Every man to his own superstitions," he said.

Captain Mauris smiled. "Would it be indiscreet to suggest that yours are non-Euclidean?"

Kobler turned away in disgust and spoke to one of his aides. "Get everyone in their contour-berths and switch the auto-announcer on. We might as well let the brain take over."

Captain Mauris made a last attempt to be helpful.

"It is well known," he said placidly, "that smooth motion never made anybody tired. But I am not so sure about smooth stillness. It may be very fatiguing. Perhaps it may even be possible for a nonexistent man to be too tired to maintain his non-existent bodily heat. Would you care for some glucose?"

Kobler did not turn around, but his shoulders shook convulsively. Captain Mauris interpreted the movement as one of silent laughter.

"One minute to deceleration point," boomed the auto-announcer.

Men with strained faces lay strapped on their contour-berths awaiting the indefinable shock of total stillness. They stared with unseeing eyes at their neighbors; at the bulkhead; at the fat ominous copper cylinder. Phylo's lips were quivering; Captain Mauris, in spite of his lighthearted precautions, felt a strange icy finger probing his heart; even Kobler's massive confidence wavered as the critical moment drew near.

"Forty-five seconds," said that damnably calm automatic voice. "Thirty seconds . . . fifteen seconds . . . ten, nine, eight, seven, six, five, four, three, two, one—zero!"

And then there was nothing: no lurch, no pressure, no sudden stress. Only a great vacancy; a sensation of utter darkness; a sharp instantaneous dream of un-being; and then only the bare memory of the dream.

In the dimensions of physical space the *Santa Maria* and all aboard her had ceased to exist. Where before a tiny metallic capsule—a caravel of explorers—had surged out from the dustlike brood of planets circling one of the innumerable suns, there was now nothing. The track of a strange silver bullet, coursing at a fantastic speed that was yet a mere snail's pace through the long deserts of the home galaxy, had stopped suddenly. There was no wreckage; there were no survivors. For what had existed in the apparent reality of space-time was now as if it had never been. . . .

Captain Mauris was alone. He was alone because there was nothing else. He was alone with the illusion of his own existence. The stillness had settled like a slow inward frost.

His premonition was justified. In a vacancy of nonsensation there was yet the overwhelming weight of a curious fatigue—as if, at the moment of deceleration, the material cosmos had suddenly become too tired to hold together. As if Mauris himself must support the tiredness of a phantom universe.

"So this is what it's like to be dead," he mumbled in a sleepy voice. He was surprised. He was pulled up with a sickening jolt. He had heard his own voice, reverberating as in an empty room. . . . The voice that followed was less of a shock than this disturbing mockery of survival.

"Captain Mauris! Captain Mauris! Soon you will be too tired to be dead, too cold to be an illusion. For you are condemned to be reborn."

It was a woman's voice, low, musical; drifting without urgency through the deep canyons of unbeing.

Mauris listened, appalled. It was a voice he recognized—the voice of a woman he might have married, a familiar voice, belonging to one he had never known.

"Who are you?" he called desperately, hearing the words echo on a wall of blackness.

There was laughter tumbling through the emptiness of stars.

"Mary Smith," said the voice, "Betty Jones and Pearl White. Marie Antoinette, Cleopatra, Helen of Troy."

"I am mad!" cried Captain Mauris. "The stars are dark, and still there is something left to dream."

"You are unborn," said the voice gently. "Have patience."

Captain Mauris tried to move and could not, for there was nothing to move, no location to be changed.

"Who am I?" he shouted wildly.

"Captain Mauris."

"There is no Captain Mauris," he yelled savagely. "He is unborn; therefore he has never lived!"

"You are learning," came the answer, softly. "You are learning that it is necessary to wait."

"Who am I?" he demanded urgently.

The laughter came like an invisible tide, sweeping him on its crest.

"Punchinello," said the voice gaily, "Prometheus, Simple Simon, Alexander the Great."

"Who am I?" he called insistently.

"You are no one. . . . Who knows? Perhaps you will become the first man. Perhaps you are waiting to be Adam."

"Then you are—"

Again the dark surge of laughter.

"I am the echo of a rib that has yet to sing."

"The rib is nowhere," said Mauris, drowsy with the effort of words. "It belongs to me, and I am unborn . . . nowhere."

"Limbo," whispered the voice.

"Nowhere," mumbled Mauris.

"Limbo," insisted the voice.

"N—where," repeated Mauris weakly, fighting the cold fatigue of stillness, the weight of unbeing.

He could feel the laughter gathering and knew that it would drown him. Desperation fought against the blind weariness sucking him into the heaving tide of sound. He tried to remember what it was like to pray.

"O God," he whispered, "if I cannot die let me become alive. Let there be light!"

Once more the laughter struck. And the whirlpool opened.

There were no stars yet, but the light came like a pallid finger, probing the interior of the stricken ship. Captain Mauris looked about him at dim shapes, and the sensation of wonder grew, while fear plucked its familiar music from his taut nerves.

There was something wrong—desperately wrong. Suddenly he understood. Everything had been reversed.

The copper cylinder, which had been bolted to the deck on the port side of the main control panel, now lay on the starboard side, its smooth fiery surface crumpled like paper. Below it, on the deck, lay beads of still-liquid copper rain.

The starboard electrochron, with its numerals reversed, now lay on the port side, above the gaping hole where the lightometer had been.

Captain Mauris turned his head to look at Kobler, but Phylo's berth now lay there in place of the physicist's. The captain knew without moving that his first officer was dead. Phylo stared at the deckhead, his features locked in a permanently vacant smile.

Glancing round at the S.F.P. chief, in Phylo's old place, Captain Mauris saw that Kobler's body was entirely relaxed. His eyes were closed, and in death he had the appearance of one who is concentrating very hard. Judging from his expression, thought Mauris, he had been trying *in extremis* to discover his error.

The navigation deck of the *Santa Maria* was a mausoleum —through the looking glass. Everything—even, as Mauris discovered, the parting in his own hair—had been reversed. He knew, without feeling the necessity to confirm it by exploration, that he was the last man alive. The *Santa Maria*, with the sole exception of its captain, was manned entirely by the dead.

"Poor devils," said Captain Mauris aloud. "Poor devils, they couldn't take the stillness. It made them too tired—dead tired!" The sound of his own voice, normal now, gave him a greater grasp on reality.

With ponderous, heavy movements, like a drunken man, he undid the straps of his contour-berth and struggled wearily to his feet. He went across to Kobler, feeling for his pulse with a forlorn hope.

"Dead tired," repeated Mauris slowly. He gazed ruefully at Kobler's pale face, set in a last frown of concentration. *"There are more things in heaven and earth, Horatio, than are dreamt of in your philosophy."*

Mauris felt neither regret nor satisfaction. There was no joy in knowing that he had the final word, that Kobler would never laugh that one away.

Presently he pulled himself together and made a cautious tour of the ship. He was as methodical as if it were a monthly routine inspection, and checked everything from the conditioner to the recycling plant. The ship, he noted ironically, was in perfect condition—but for two small details: the planetary and stellar drives were completely wrecked. Apart from the fact that the landing retard and auxiliary brake rockets were intact, the *Santa Maria* was at the mercy of normal gravity fields.

There were only two reasonable possibilities. She might coast merrily in the void forever, or drop eventually into a sun. The alternative was too improbable for consideration, for the chances of falling into the gravity field of a hospitable planet were several billion billion to one.

Finally Captain Mauris was confronted with the task he had been subconsciously shirking. Steeling himself against a paralyzing reluctance, he climbed up into the astrodome and looked at the stars.

He did not need star charts to tell him that this was not the home galaxy. As he gazed at the sharp unfamiliar patterns, an already tight band seemed to constrict around his heart. Perhaps Kobler had succeeded. Perhaps the galaxy M 81 had been entered by a terrene ship for the first time. Much good it would do the United Space Corporation!

With a grim smile Mauris recalled that final paragraph of the ship's articles. *If the master should satisfy himself, and the authorized scientists concerned, that the danger factor is sufficient* . . . It was really very funny! Probably sixteen hundred thousand light-years away, on a speck of cosmic dust, the Field Testing Executive had already set up their officious court of inquiry to consider possible reasons for the loss of their experimental ship.

Then suddenly he realized that if the *Santa Maria* had indeed reached M 81, the planet Earth was not only sixteen hundred thousand light-years away, it was also sixteen hundred thousand years ago.

He had a sudden image of the Field Testing Executive with apelike faces, sitting and jabbering pompously around a mud pool in some prehistoric steamy jungle. And Mauris laughed. He laughed loudly, raucously. He laughed until he cried—until weariness, in a sudden triumph, toppled him senseless on the deck. And there he lay, sleeping like a child whose nightmares materialize only when he is awake.

He never knew how long he slept. He was eventually wakened by a sharp, agonizing pain in his stomach. At last, through a fog of bewilderment, he recognized it as hunger. He staggered along to the mess-deck and operated the food-delivery controls. A minute and a half later he pulled a nicely roasted chicken, complete with potatoes and green peas, from the electronic cooker. He ate ravenously, and followed it up with cheese and biscuits, coffee and liqueur brandy. The brandy was a special bottle that had been optimistically saved for a celebration banquet. As he sipped it luxuriously, Captain Mauris thought of all the guests who were unable to attend. Gravely he included Kobler, Phylo and all the rest of the *Santa Maria's* personnel in the toast: "Absent friends!" Then he took the old corncob pipe from his pocket and lit up. Presently Captain Mauris was feeling almost human.

He spent the rest of the "day" launching dead bodies into space. Wearing his combination pressure suit, Captain Mauris lugged them one after another through the airlock and gave them a shove. Kobler, Phylo and the rest went sailing smoothly out into the starry darkness. To each one Captain Mauris gave a personal farewell, as if he might have been expecting an answer.

Presently the *Santa Maria* was surrounded by a slowly dispersing shoal of flying corpses whose presence was only inferred where they blotted out the background of unwinking stars.

Finally when all the unwelcome furniture had been jettisoned, the captain went back to the navigation deck and made the ship accelerate for three seconds on her auxiliary rockets, thus leaving the shoal behind. Having accomplished this disagreeable task Mauris felt much better.

But as he clambered into the astrodome for a further check on the unfamiliar star positions it dawned on him that he had probably looked on a human face for the last time.

Nine "days" later, by the ship's electrochron, Captain Mauris became convinced that he would not have to wait much longer. The star on the port bow had grown to the size of a penny. Presently it would grow to the size of a football. Presently the *Santa Maria* and her captain would reach the end of their journey—in the purification of celestial fire.

He had already resigned himself calmly to his destiny and was, in truth, a little pleased that Fate had arranged a definite appointment with death for him. It was certainly preferable to drifting aimlessly for months, waiting until the food supply was exhausted, waiting until he went mad or plucked up enough courage to make the appointment on his own initiative.

The condemned man continued to eat hearty breakfasts, and settled down to enjoy, in his last days, what he had never yet experienced throughout his life—a period of sustained leisure. A period of rest and tranquility, interrupted by nothing more serious than the push-button operations necessary for providing first-class meals.

Captain Mauris spent more and more time in the ship's library, projecting the microfilms of books he had never had the time to read. Intuitively he went to the old writers, ranging at a leisurely pace through fiction and nonfiction, from Plato to Dickens, from Homer to H. G. Wells. He also browsed through the Bible, and amused himself by translating its profound convictions into the sort of language that Kobler used.

By the eighteenth day Captain Mauris was confused, disappointed, excited and afraid. The now brilliantly blinding sun had changed its position from port bow to starboard quarter. Its place on the port bow had been taken by what seemed to be a green marble. Captain Mauris knew it was not another sun and tried desperately not to allow himself to

110

hope that it might be a habitable planet. Better to die by falling into an alien sun than survive, a castaway on an unknown planet in some alien galaxy. His reason said so but his emotions remained unconvinced.

It was then, for no reason at all, that he suddenly remembered the voice and the dreamlike laughter he had experienced in the total darkness, the absolute stillness of the galactic jump.

And Captain Mauris had a premonition.

On the twenty-fifth day the possibility became a certainty. The *Santa Maria* was falling toward the green planet. There remained the problem of choice between two courses of action. Captain Mauris could either allow the ship to continue her free fall until she vapourized on hitting the atmosphere—if any—or exploded on ground impact, or else he could apply the auxiliary brake rockets and the landing retard, thus making a bid for survival.

The period of tranquillity was over; he was in a state of chronic indecision.

He was afraid in the very core of his being. He was afraid to make up his mind. The captain went uncertainly to the mess-deck, seeking consolation and enlightenment in the liqueur brandy. He did not find it.

Eventually he was drawn back to the navigation deck as by a magnet. He climbed into the astrodome and regarded the green planet. It was expanding rapidly, almost visibly. With trembling fingers Captain Mauris adjusted the manual telescope. He gazed through it at a startlingly close panorama of oceans, continents and islands. He stared hypnotically for a while and felt the beads of cold moisture grow on his forehead.

At last he came down and went to drink more brandy. It solved nothing, because he was still sober enough to face the choice.

Suddenly he could stand it no more. He lurched unsteadily to the navigation deck, reached the control panel and threw in three switches almost simultaneously. Reflex-radar, altimeter and positioning gyro were immediately synchronized with the auto-pilot. Whether the reversed instruments functioned correctly or not Mauris neither knew nor cared. He had rid himself of an intolerable weight. He had made a decision.

Immediately he who had accepted so much responsibility in his career felt an overwhelming need to escape the responsibility of attempting to survive. He fled to the library and, forcing himself to try to forget the decision, placed a random microfilm in the book projector. It was *The Golden Ass* of Apuleius.

He looked at the words and they had no meaning for him. He was too busy awaiting the shock of the first automatic blast of the auxiliary brake rockets.

After an eternity of hours that seemed years he felt a sharp surge as the motors produced a field of double gravity, piling on the ship's own synthetic 1/3 G force.

Mauris fell sideways from his chair and lay on the bulkhead, groaning heavily. The rocket burst lasted five seconds and he felt crushed by its relentless force. Abruptly it ended; he slithered painfully to the deck.

Then the old habits reasserted themselves. The master's place in a power maneuver was on the navigation deck. Captain Mauris picked himself up and made his way forward.

The second automatic power maneuver hit him before he could reach a contour-berth. A field of 5 G slammed him against the bulkhead of the navigation deck. He had fallen sideways about ten feet. He lay there spreadeagled, unconscious.

The auto-pilot had positioned the ship accurately. The ship's attitude, controlled by the gyro-manipulator, had brought the green planet dead astern; and with rockets blazing the *Santa Maria* dropped backward to that rapidly expanding surface. On the screens of the external visulators, the silvery shapes of mountains and hills, of rivers and forests leaped into a growing reality. The fleecy shapes of clouds passed like fantastic birds.

But Captain Mauris lay inert against the bulkhead, the accelerating G force crushing his unconscious body to the hard metal.

He awoke with every muscle aching from the tremendous stress of ordinary physical deceleration, but he awoke with a sensation of profound peace.

He picked himself up and climbed into the astrodome. The stars were no longer sharp, unwinking points against a backcloth of jet. They twinkled, dancing to the whim of atmosphere.

Looking down, Captain Mauris felt his heart thump violently. The *Santa Maria* had made a perfect automatic landing on what appeared, in the semi-darkness, to be smooth

112

grassland. A few yards away he thought he saw dimly the ripple of running water.

The United Space Corporation had laid down a cautious and definitive procedure for the exploration of strange planets. But, as Mauris told himself lightly, the *United Space Corporation* would not begin to exist even in its own galaxy for another sixteen hundred thousand years.

Casting discretion aside Captain Mauris made his way aft toward the airlock. He seized a combination pressure suit and climbed into it impatiently. Then he entered the pressure chamber. He closed the door behind him and threw the switch. The needle remained steady, indicating that the external pressure—the planetary atmosphere—was at par.

Captain Mauris was surprised. He began to feel that it was part of some obliging dream. He pressed a luminous button on the bulkhead and a heavy door of the entry-port swung open. The captain took a nylon ladder from its locker and secured one end to the stanchions of the entry-port. He tossed out the bundle of ladder and watched it drop through the misty atmosphere. Then slowly he climbed down.

Captain Mauris stood still and gazed at the terrain through a deceptive half-light. What he could see of it was so reassuringly normal as to be quite improbable. It might have been country in the temperate zones of Earth.

He tried to think of the fantastic chances against landing on such a planet after the *Santa Maria* had crippled both her stellar and planetary drives in the extra-galactic jump. Logically there was no chance. What had happened was merely impossible.

"Luck," thought Captain Mauris. "Or is it something else?"

With sudden inexplicable determination he tried to tempt Fate for the last time. He released the safety valve on his pressure suit. Nothing happened. With an audible laugh of triumph and amazement he began to take off the headpiece. Presently he stepped out of the pressure suit, his oxygen cylinder unneeded.

Captain Muris stood on an unknown planet and took in the unmistakable scents of summer. He felt drunk—drunk on the sheer fantasy of reality. As he gazed about him he saw, over a patch of woodland, gray streaks of light pushing back the darkness, dulling the stars. And fifty yards from the spaceship, he discerned the edge of a stream whose quiet murmur seemed suddenly to communicate with his awakened sense of hearing.

Giving a wild cry of pleasure Mauris forgot all about

113

space-frame physicists and the extra-galactic jump. He ran swiftly to the banks of the stream, tore off his stale clothes and waded into the dark, refreshing water.

And as he bathed the intensity of light grew over the distant trees.

At last he came out of the stream, refreshed and exhilarated. He felt a warm breeze against his body, felt the blood coursing more rapidly through his veins.

He did not bother to dress, but walked wonderingly toward the increasing light.

The vault of darkness was being pushed slowly back, while the stars seemed to slip behind an invisible curtain.

Captain Mauris watched the landscape come quietly to life. Then he looked up at the sky.

"And darkness," said Captain Mauris, as he gazed at the fading stars, "darkness was upon the face of the deep."

He stood there, feeling the years roll back, feeling the vitality of youth drive back some secret winter. At length he turned around to look at the spaceship, to assure himself of the reality of the journey. There was nothing to be seen. The thin vein of water flowed quietly through vacant land.

Surprised at his own calmness, his lack of distress, he turned again toward the patch of trees. And from the direction that he would learn to call east there rose the crimson edge of a new sun.

He remembered then and suddenly understood the message of a woman's voice in a dream of absolute stillness.

THE ENLIGHTENED ONES

Lukas threw a rapid glance at the bank of instruments on the navigation panel. Velocity had stabilized at thirty thousand kilometers. with a constant altitude of three hundred and fifty. Down below—and it was certainly a relief to use the concept "below" once again after several thousand hours of star flight—the red-gold continental masses of Fomalhaut Three swung slowly along their apparent rotation.

Soon the starship *Henri Poincare* would make its first free-fall transit over the night side of the planet. For all practical purposes this was the end of the outward journey. Allowing his gaze to return to the procession of continents and emerald-green oceans on the surface of Fomalhaut Three, Captain Lukas felt a faint surge of anticipatory pleasure.

"Orbit maneuver concluded," he said softly, over his shoulder. "O.D. shut down."

Duluth, the engineer, who was standing expectantly by the control pedestal, stooped down and threw back his master switch. He watched the red power needle slowly fall to zero. Then he stood up and yawned.

"Orbit drive shut down," he remarked drowsily. "And now I'm going to get me some sleep. Do you know how long we've been awake, skipper?"

Lukas turned from the observation screen and grinned. "What's the matter, Joe? Feeling old?"

Duluth stretched and yawned even more profoundly. "In case you haven't noticed, we've been on duty more than two days. A man gets just a little fatigued after staying awake maybe sixty hours."

Lukas watched him with red-rimmed eyes. "Don't worry," he said. "I noticed."

At that moment they heard steps on the companion ladder. A couple of seconds later Alsdorf, the geophysicist, poked his head through the hatch. He looked fresh, almost bursting with energy; but then he hadn't needed to stay awake for the maneuvers.

"You two look like death," said Alsdorf pleasantly. "Come on down to the mess-deck. Tony is fixing cocoa and sandwiches."

"The hell with sandwiches," said Duluth. "I want to sleep."

Alsdoirf beamed. "Cocoa first, then a sedative. You'll need it with all those action tablets you've taken."

Lukas said, "Well, we got here, Kurt. Now you can earn your living. From here on I'm a spectator."

The intercom crackled. "What's the matter?" complained an indignant voice. "There's a gallon of hot cocoa waiting for you. Want me to recycle it?"

"Recycle yourself," growled Duluth. "O.K. We're on our way, Tony."

With Alsdorf leading, they went down to the mess-deck. Tony Chirico, a dapper Italian biochemist who looked as if he ought to have been a barber, greeted Lukas with a toothy smile.

"So you got us here, Mike. Somebody ought to make a speech about it. Have a sandwich."

"What's in 'em?' asked Duluth suspiciously, as he grabbed a pint flask of cocoa and anchored himself to a bench.

'Bombay Duck," said Chirico, "same as usual."

115

Duluth gave a mirthless laugh. "Hydroponics garbage *a la carte*."

Captain Lukas sat down and sipped his cocoa. He gazed at the observation panel and saw the dark side of Fomalhaut Three turning slowly into view.

"We're a fine bunch of heroes," he remarked. "With the imaginative capacity of bedbugs. Here we knock a hole through space and find a system that nobody has ever seen before, and what do we do? We sit on our backsides, drink cocoa and grumble about the food. For all we know, this planet we're riding might have a civilization that'd make all Earth cultures look like a cretin's nightmare."

"A virgin planet," said Alsdorf, with an avaricious gleam in his eye. "Trans-Solar Chemicals will set up an independent station here . . . with one Kurt Alsdorf as director."

"A virgin planet," echoed Chirico with a sardonic grin. "I think we shall awaken her—gently."

"Can it," mumbled Duluth, slumping over the table. "You got virgins on the brain."

"You don't think we're going to find any intelligent owners down there?" asked Lukas.

Alsdorf lit a cigarette. "Face the facts, Mike. In the last two decades seventeen new planets have been listed. The highest animal life discovered so far was the three-legged pseudo-wolf on Procyon Five. You could train it to fetch sticks, and that was all."

Lukas took a good swig of his cocoa. "Well, it's got to happen some day."

Chirico laughed. "Sure, everything has to happen some day. Give a monkey with a typewriter enough time, and he'll rewrite Shakespeare with genuine improvements."

Lukas shrugged. "A few hundred years ago men thought that Earth was unique. Now they think only the human race is unique. I hope I'm still around when bright boys like you get the big surprise."

Alsdorf prodded Duluth and was rewarded with a volley of snores and grunts. "Joe is no longer with us,' he remarked. "We ought to put him to bed. You, too, Mike. We need you wide awake when we go down to the surface to hunt out the supermen." He gave a hearty laugh.

"Enjoy yourself," grinned Lukas. "Now it's your turn to lose some sleep. How long will it take to select a touch-down point?"

The geophysicist stared absently through the observation panel. "Nine-tenths water," he murmured almost to himself.

116

"A good continental survey should take about a hundred hours, but we can probably select a useful area in a quarter of that time."

Captain Lukas stood up and grabbed Duluth unceremoniously by the collar. "Give me a hand with the body, Tony." He turned to Alsdorf. "Don't be soft-hearted, Kurt. Tumble me out if anything unusual crops up." With Chirico's help he maneuvered the still-unconscious Duluth toward the doorway.

Three minutes later Duluth was installed in his bunk, and Mike Lukas headed for his own cubicle. Curiously, he had lost a great deal of his tiredness. As he settled himself luxuriously on his narrow mattress he reached for a book and a packet of cigarettes.

Chirico watched him, amazed. "You've been awake all this time, Mike, and you want to read? You're crazy. Why don't you take a nice pill?"

"On your way, nursie. I'm just relaxing. I'll doze off in a while."

The small Italian made an economical gesture signifying a verdict of insanity and returned to the mess-deck. He found Alsdorf intently studying a pocket slide-rule and a scrap of paper on which was a rough pencil sketch of the hemispheres of Fomalhaut Three, and a sequence of calculations.

"I'm beginning to think Mike takes his Buddhism seriously," remarked Chirico, helping himself to another sandwich.

Alsdorf looked up and raised an eyebrow. The Italian took a large bite of his sandwich, then continued: "He's been awake for fifty-six hours and now he's busy reading *The Way To Nirvana.* Seems to me he's halfway there already."

The geophysicist registered a superior smile. "Overtired, Tony. But I have noticed that most of these professional space pilots affect some sort of religion. A convenient safety valve for irrational fears."

Tony thought it over for a few seconds. "In the last analysis I'm a Catholic," he said finally. "We all need something."

Alsdorf picked up his slide-rule. "Not all of us, Tony. I'm with the mechanists. The universe is clockwork, all cause and effect. Frankly, I don't know how you people ever reconcile superstition with science. You and Mike must be intellectual schizoids."

Chirico smiled. "You're a computer, Kurt. Computers don't go to heaven."

The geophysicist stood up. "At the moment I'm more interested in going to the navigation deck. And so are you, you tabu-ridden primitive. There's work to be done. The sooner it's done, the sooner we climb a little higher in *Trans-Solar Chemicals.*"

Chirico said suddenly, "Kurt, what do you want out of life?"

"Power," said Alsdorf calmly. "And you?"

"I don't know. I'm still thinking about it. Maybe I just want a sense of direction—to do something that's worth doing."

"You want power," said Alsdorf confidently. "Everybody does. It's the life force—the mainspring of dynamic evolution."

The Italian beamed. "O.K., Mr. Mephistopheles, let's go and be dynamic about that landing site."

They went out into the alleyway and along to the navigation deck, the magnetic bars of their shoes clanking eerily through the silent ship.

The survey, conducted in Olympian remoteness three hundred and fifty kilometers over Fomalhaut Three, proceeded with almost startling efficiency. Visibility was excellent, and it was the first time in Kurt Alsdorf's experience that none of the delicate probing instruments broke down at the critical moment. Presently a stereo-radar, vegetometer and other probe instruments united their findings to give a clear and detailed assessment of conditions in the tropical zone. It was even possible to do some useful work with the manual telescope.

After fourteen hours Chirico looked up from his contourgrams and said: "This place is better than Earth, by damn!"

Even the impassive Alsdorf could not screen his excitement. "Tony, it's the best yet: near-terrestrial temperatures, a one-to-six oxygen ratio, a four-thousand-kilometer vegetation belt—why, with these conditions we can—"

"If I were you I'd sit on the hysteria long enough to find out whether anyone is already squatting on Fomalhaut Three."

The two men turned round to find that Lukas had quietly appeared through the companion hatch.

Alsdorf grinned sheepishly. "Hello, Mike. Still thinking in terms of supermen?"

"Maybe, maybe not."

Chirico said, "By all the laws, you should still be unconscious."

Lukas walked over to the chart bench and began to inspect the fruits of research. "My, my," he said dryly, "just like Earth before we remodeled it with the hydrogen bombs. Now we'll have to start all over again."

Alsdorf waved a large telephoto print in front of his face. "Here's the landing area—as from an altitude of three thousand meters. What do you think of that?"

"Looks fine."

"It's got everything, Mike," said Chirico eagerly. "It's the classic survey block—a hundred square kilometers of desert, foothills, river and seaboard. Everything from dense vegetation to bare rockface. Think of the ecology."

"*You* think of it. I'll concentrate on getting us down there. . . . When will you be ready to move, Kurt?"

The geophysicist put the telephoto print down on the bench and watched Lukas speculatively. "What's the matter, Mike, is this trip going sour on you? Maybe you need a tonic."

"Don't we all?" Lukas gazed moodily through the observation panel. "Me, you and *homo sapiens*. We need a new perspective, a revitalized set of values. Space travel arrived when we were getting mentally and emotionally flabby. We reacted to it as to a shot in the arm. But so far all we've done is get nowhere—a lot quicker. We've found seventeen new planets and we haven't learned a thing. We just grab what we want and push on to the next Garden of Eden. We're a bunch of traveling snakes in the grass."

Alsdorf shrugged. "You mix a nice line in metaphors, but they don't mean anything."

"There's one consolation," said Chirico with a grin. "None of us space snakes has come across any Adam and Eve set-up yet."

"No," said Lukas somberly. "But we will—and then, God help them."

Alsdorf climbed up into the astrodome and began to re-adjust the manual telescope. "I'll have the rest of the data ready in about six hours, Mike—if you can drop the Garden of Eden *motif* long enough to plan the touch-down." His tone was heavy with sarcasm.

"On with the good work," said Lukas. "I'll go and kick Duluth out of bed and get him to check the volatility tubes."

He disappeared from the companion ladder.

"Do you think Mike is off his trolley?" asked Chirico thoughtfully.

Alsdorf squinted down the telescope. "Not yet. He's just

119

got an ingrowing conscience. Space pilots don't last very long, you know."

The Italian began to reset the stereo-radar. "What the hell," he said softly. "We're all expendable."

Nine hours later the *Henri Poincare* swung slowly out of orbit into the first vast circuit of an oblique descent spiral. After fifteen minutes it hit the outer fringes of the stratosphere, and the four occupants, each strapped in a contour-berth on the navigation deck, prepared to endure an agonizing switchback as the ship reduced its velocity by frictional impact on the thin layers of air.

Lukas, relieved of all responsibility by the automatic decisions of the electronic touch-down pilot, managed to achieve some degree of indifference to the tremendous pressures set up by deceleration. Long experience had enabled him to develop a kind of mental block against the worst discomforts of a bouncy touch-down maneuver. His head lay on the pillow facing an observation panel, and during the odd moments when the G forces eased sufficiently to let him use his eyes, he could see an expanding arc of Fomalhaut Three swinging crazily against the jet backcloth of space.

In spite of having a respectable number of voyages behind him, Duluth always took the touch-down drop badly. He would strain instinctively and uselessly against the relentless forces that crushed him down. As the *Henri Poincare* plowed jerkily into the thicker layers of air, Duluth felt the deadly ache of resistance tearing at his muscles, and impotently muttered a broken stream of obscenities.

Alsdorf and Chirico, both comparative novices of the touch-down ordeal, had taken the sensible precaution of putting themselves completely to sleep. But even though they were unconscious their bodies sagged and contorted as if they were twitched by invisible strings.

Presently the ship hit the atmosphere proper. This time the pressure was unendurable. Lukas and Duluth blacked out simultaneously. When they next opened their eyes the pain was already fading from their bodies. They became conscious of a luxurious feeling of peace. The *Henri Poincare* had made a perfect touch-down.

Duluth shook his head in momentary bewilderment. "I almost swallowed my bloody tongue," he remarked hoarsely. He looked around and saw that Lukas was already unbuckling his straps. Alsdorf and Chirico had stopped twitching, but they were still unconscious. "Look at the sleeping beauties," added Duluth, feeling better. "How long does that lullaby stuff last?"

Lukas stood up and stretched. He winced suddenly as his back muscles, still unaccustomed to the release of tension, gave a sharp twinge.

"They should be with us inside half an hour. . . . Come on, Joe, let's take a look around the next stamping ground of Trans-Solar Chemicals."

He scrambled up into the observation dome and took his first close look at the new planet.

"What's it like?" called Duluth as he struggled impatiently with the network of safety belts. "Anything startling?"

Lukas was amazed. "Holy smoke! Apart from the colors, this could be South America or the African coast!" His voice shook with excitement.

"Jesus," said Duluth. "Maybe we took the wrong turning and blasted ourselves back into the System." He hurried up the short ladder and stood by Lukas's side.

From their observation point in the nose of the ship, more than seventy meters above ground level, they commanded a panoramic view of the landing area.

The *Henri Poincare* had come to rest on a broad sand belt. About five kilometers to the planetary east, the calm emerald-green ocean lay flat as a mirror under a misty, somewhat yellowish sky. On the opposite side of the ship, a kilometer or so to the west, a bright blue-green forest line rose abruptly from the red sand. Nothing moved anywhere; but far away on the sand belt was a colony of dark spots that proved, on inspection by the telescope, to be a flock of resting birds—something like terrestrial gulls.

High above, the noon sun contrived to filter its oddly relaxing light through the even layer of cloud. The star, Fomalhaut, was a thousand million miles away; but its intense radiation bathed the third planet with sunlight almost equal to the tropical brilliance found on Earth.

"Well, what do you know?" exclaimed Duluth, after several seconds of fascinated silence. "Isn't that something! What's the atmosphere like, anybody find out?"

"Tony says we can use it, but better be careful than sorry . . . . How about letting the ladder down while Kurt and Tony are finishing their beauty sleep?"

"I'm on my way," said Duluth. "Think I'll jump into a pressure suit and stroll around."

"You'll be all right with a respiration mask," Lukas assured him. "The pressure is slightly under one atmos."

Duluth climbed down from the observation dome, kissed his fingers archly to the unconscious scientists and disappeared down the companion ladder. Presently Lukas heard him manipulating the airlock.

Lukas stayed in the dome for a while, gazing around him. The vague uneasiness he had felt about Fomalhaut Three intensified. He was not normally a superstitious man, or given to premonitions; and his uneasiness was hard to analyze.

As a veteran of three other planetary investigations he was mentally prepared for any reasonable physical hazards that might be expected. But although Lukas sensed some kind of threat hidden in the almost conventional landscape of Fomalhaut Three, he felt oddly confident that it wasn't physical.

As his eyes strayed idly over the forest line he thought he detected some kind of movement, but by the time he got the telescope focused there was nothing to be seen. Probably, he told himself, it was some trick of the peculiar yellow light.

Somnolent groans from down below indicated that Alsdorf and Chirico were returning to consciousness. He went down the ladder to help them with their straps.

"Devil take it," grumbled the small Italian, blinking painfully, "I have the mother and father of all hangovers."

"Swallow a pill. You'll feel better.

With a hand on his forehead Alsdorf gently worked his head up and down. He seemed surprised when it didn't fall off. "What's the situation?" he asked.

Lukas jerked a thumb toward the observation dome. "Too good to be true. See for yourself."

"Any signs of life?"

"Birds, I think, but too far away for detail to show up."

"Well, well. That's an excellent start. Maybe we'll find something better than a three-legged pseudo-wolf, eh, Mike?"

"Maybe."

The two scientists went up into the observation dome. Lucas watched them, then said, "Joe's already stretching his legs. Can you see him?"

Chirico laughed. "For a moment I thought he was the welcome committee."

Lukas said, "I could use a drink before we go outside. If you need me I'll be on the mess-deck." He went down the companion ladder.

Ten minutes later Alsdorf and Chirico joined him. They

122

sat around the table, sipping hot coffee, enjoying the feel of an almost normal gravity pull and discussing plans for tackling the survey block. Alsdorf, as the senior representative of Trans-Solar Chemicals, was busy making out duty lists.

Suddenly there was a commotion on the lower deck. Then the sound of heavy metallic boots on the main ladder. The three men jumped up and went to the hatch. They met Duluth on his way up. He was wearing a pressure suit. As soon as he saw them he pressed the emergency release and whipped off his headpiece.

"Apes!" he panted. "Bloody big ones!"

"Where?" snapped Alsdorf.

"Half a kilometer away. There's a troop of them, fifteen maybe twenty, heading toward us from the forest."

Chirico was almost bouncing with excitement. "This gets better and better. It looks like we really found something this time."

The three of them hurried into pressure suits, while Duluth picked up a couple of machine pistols to deal with any mis-understandings that might arise. Then they went down to the airlock. By the time they had got through the entry-port and climbed down the landing ladder the approaching troop was less than a hundred meters away.

Duluth and Alsdorf held the machine pistols firmly at their hips. "Ain't this joyful?" remarked Duluth over his personal radio. "Hey, they got bundles with 'em. What's the betting they're going to pelt us with king-size coconuts?"

"Anthropoids!" exclaimed Chirico incredulously. "By all that's holy, we've found anthropoids on the first touch-down. . . . No, by heaven, they're not anthropoids—they're hominids! Look at the size of those heads!"

Lukas was staring through his vizor intently. His eyes had not yet adjusted to the strange light of Fomalhaut Three; but as the troop came closer, moving at a queer half-trot, he saw that their limbs were pale and hairless but their faces were half hidden under dark, shaggy manes.

"The major difference between us and them," he said quietly, "is a haircut."

"Plus another small detail," said Alsdorf with some com-placency. "We happen to be civilized."

Lukas gave a dry laugh. "That's our story. We might as well stick to it."

Fifteen paces away the troop fanned out into a semicircle and came to a halt. At a signal from one in the center they placed their burdens down on the sand and waited expect-

123

antly. Men and hominids gazed at each other. Both groups seemed reluctant to make the first move.

Lukas and his companions saw that the inhabitants of Fomalhaut Three were almost uniformly tall—each of them about two inches higher than Alsdorf, who was the tallest of the terrenes. They were massive-chested creatures with hunched shoulders and long sinewy arms. Their toes splayed out uneasily, as if they were more accustomed to gripping branches than supporting those tough, wiry bodies in even balance. Their faces—what could be seen of them under the matting of coarse hair—were almost Neanderthal, with broad, flared nostrils, thick lips, receding foreheads, and an occasional glimpse of dark eyes under bushy brows.

Presently one of them, whose hair was lighter and thinner than the rest, stepped out from the group and raised his right arm forward, level with the shoulder, as if in greeting. He began to work his lips.

Encased in their pressure suits the terrenes could hear no sound. But Lukas suddenly decided that it was worth risking a few alien bugs to hear what Neanderthal Man, Fomalhaut Three version, had to say. He took off his headpiece.

"*Czanyas*," said the hominid, touching his own chest. Then, pointing at the terrenes, he added: "*Olye ma nye kran czanyas.*"

Lukas took a couple of steps forward and repeated the word "*czanyas*" experimentally with his finger pointing at the hominid.

The whole troop made a rumbling noise in their throats, and lips curved in broad grins. Encouraged, Lukas thumped his own chest. "*Olye ma nye kran czanyas?*" He displayed his bewilderment with exaggerated gestures.

The old hominid pointed to the sky. "*Olye*" Then he pointed to Lukas, Alsdorf, Duluth and Chirico in turn. "*Czanyas. . . . Olye ma nye kran czanyas.*"

Duluth had taken his headpiece off. "What does the old bird say, Mike?"

"In case we didn't notice it," said Lukas with a grin, "he's pointing out the difference between us and them—I think. They are men, and we are men of the ship of the sky, or something like that."

The old hominid turned and made a small hand signal to his own kind. One at a time they came forward and laid their presents at the feet of the terrenes. Then they returned to the semicircle and squatted. Presently each of the terrenes had at his feet a pile of assorted fruits of varying shapes, sizes and colors. Chirico, unable to restrain his interest, took off his headpiece and sat down to examine his pile. He began to sort out the local equivalents of melon, grapes, oranges, nuts and even maize.

Only Alsdorf remained unrelaxed, still wearing his head-piece, still covering the hominids with his machine pistol.

Lukas examined his own pile of fruit, then with much gesture and patient repetition, managed to make the hominids understand that he and his companions were grateful. Finally he turned to Duluth. "Better make this mutual. What can we give 'em, Joe?"

Duluth grinned. "How about a machine pistol or a gas bomb?"

But Lukas wasn't in the mood for humor. "They'll be getting the benefits of civilization soon enough. Better break out a few plastic bowls. Jump to it!"

"Aye aye, skipper. Keep your shirt on." Duluth went back into the ship and emerged a few minutes later with an armful of utensils, which he presented to the hominids, gravely wishing each one in turn a Merry Christmas.

For the next hour or so Lukas and Chirico concentrated on establishing the meaning of various words. Even Alsdorf became sufficiently interested to take off his headpiece and join in. They discovered that *solyenas* was food: *czanyas solyenas ra,* man eats food. They learned that *koshevo* was the word for water; *ilshevo* the word for land; and *lashevo* the word for air. From this they finally elucidated that *olye* was not the sky but the sun.

And while these language concepts were being established the sun sank slowly down the yellowish sky until it hung just over the forest line. The hominids then indicated that they wished to go back to the forest, but would return again "when the sun swam out of the ocean."

"Mahrata," said the old, grizzled leader, raising his arm. *"Olye kalengo, czanyas kalengo. Olye rin koshevo, da czanyas va."*

"Me, too," grinned Duluth. "What's he saying, Mike?"

"He says: 'Farewell. Sun sleeps, men sleep. Sun swims from water, then men return.' "

The four terrenes watched the troop of hominids make their way back across the sand belt to the now darkening forest line. Then they went back into the ship, taking most of the fruit with them and dumping it in the laboratory for Chirico's further attention.

The brief but tremendous stress of touch-down, followed

by the equally tremendous discovery that Fomalhaut Three was inhabited by manlike beings, had almost drained them of emotional and intellectual energy. They were tired and, to their surpise, ravenously hungry.

However there was still some daylight left, and Alsdorf suggested that they rig up the cargo derrick and lower the caterpillar tractor to the ground in readiness for the first survey trip. But by the time the derrick was ready to take the tractor it was too dark to see what they were doing. Duluth went up to the navigation deck and swung out three searchlights, focusing them on the ground immediately below the derrick. For another ten or fifteen minutes the men worked in silence, lugging the tractor out of the bowels of the ship and hooking it up to the derrick with hiduminium hawsers. At last they lowered away, and had the satisfaction of knowing that the first survey party could push off as soon as the sun rose.

"By the Lord Harry, I'm dead on my feet," panted Duluth as he stared down at the tractor in the pale circular glare of the arc-lights.

Chirico wiped the sweat from his forehead. "Bet I could eat one of our tame hominids raw."

"I have a suggestion," said Lukas. "Iced beer and chicken. Anybody with me?"

There was a minor stampede to the mess-deck.

Throughout a long, luxurious meal, discussion centred mainly upon the hominids and the possibility of Fomalhaut Three's containing more highly developed cultures. Of the four of them, Alsdorf was the least interested in what he referred to as "the organic curiosities of the planet." Being one of the star geophysicists of Trans-Solar Chemicals, his preoccupation was solely with the mineral content of the planet, how best it could be exploited and the resulting products transported to the solar system.

"Do not forget," he said dryly, "that we are here to look for rare metals, not to investigate the indigenous life forms. The hominids are interesting but we must not let them sidetrack us. On the other hand, if there are possibilities of large scale mining they may provide a convenient labor force. Otherwise—"

Lukas slammed his beer mug down. "Kurt, there are times when you make me sick. These poor bastards have a right to their own existence. I'm damned if I'd see them turned into a bunch of coolies so that Trans-Solar can double its dividends. Don't you have any conscience?"

Alsdorf grinned. "My duty toward my neighbor," he said slyly, "is surely my duty toward my fellow human beings. If the situation demanded it I would not hesitate to exploit these creatures for the benefit of humanity. We should, of course, civilize them in the process."

"Bluebells to both of you," drawled Duluth, with an inane grin. "Quit arguin' about what ain't happenin', and for Chrissake have another beer. . . . I wonder if those long-haired boys got any idea how to make wallop? Thash the way to shivilishe 'em—teash 'em to make corn brandy and shay shir to the nishe zhentlemen from shpace."

Next day at dawn the hominids returned, bringing with them more presents, only this time the presents were such as to make Alsdorf's eyes practically pop out of his head.

Nobody was awake when they arrived, so they squatted patiently outside the *Henri Poincare,* nursing their presents and chanting a kind of tuneless psalm, either to the ship or its occupants.

Lukas was the first to go down to them. He saw that their presents consisted of small whitish metal drinking bowls, crudely ornamented, and it occurred to him that these were offered in exchange for the colored plastic bowls that had been presented to the hominids the day before.

The old one who had previously done the talking again stepped out and opened the ceremony.

"Mahrata-nua," he said. *"Olye rin a koshevo, e czanyas va kala mu omeso."* He touched the bowl he was holding to the center of his forehead, then held it out to Lukas.

Lukas had a peculiar feeling. For one odd moment he had the conviction that the hominids were staging an elaborate joke—the sort of joke that sophisticated adults might rig for the benefit of credulous children. Then he met the innocent gaze of the old hominid and the feeling passed.

He took the bowl and was still busy expressing his thanks in mime and language when Alsdorf came down. The geophysicist was immediately presented with a bowl himself. With a brief gesture and a patronizing smile for the old one he suddenly forgot everything and began to examine the bowl intently. He took a small knife from his pocket and scratched the surface. Then he took out a lens and peered at the scratch through it. Uttering a sharp exclamation he hurried back into the ship. Five minutes later he returned, pale and trembling.

"Mike, do you know what this thing is made of?" He

stared at the bowl in his hand with an expression of sheer disbelief.

"Haven't a clue," said Lukas calmly. "You tell me."

"Platinum," croaked Alsdorf. "Solid platinum! We've just been presented with a small fortune."

Though it was obviously impossible for the hominids to understand what Alsdorf was saying they grinned broadly, as if they were delighted with his excitement—or as if their subtle private joke was a big success.

While Alsdorf was assuring himself that the bowl Lukas held was also made of platinum, Duluth and Chirico appeared. They, too, went through the presentation ceremony.

"Well, I'll be sugared," said Duluth, clutching his bowl tightly. "Pure platinum, by Hades! Now suppose we fix up a little trading post—plastics for platinum, and fair exchange is no robbery. We wouldn't have to stay in business long. You know, I always planned on buying a little estate in the south of France when I get too old for space travel. Now, I'll just buy me the south of France."

Chirico looked glum. "The moment we hit the solar system," he said, "Trans-Solar will step in. Before you know it the bottom will have dropped out of the platinum market."

"We'll make a killing with the first load," said Duluth happily. "Think I'll buy Switzerland, as well—just for the winter sports."

Lukas grinned. "This ship is under charter," he remarked. "Read your articles, son. All cargo belong to Trans-Solar."

Meanwhile the old hominid began another speech. After much effort on both sides it became clear that he was offering the hospitality of his village.

Alsdorf said, "We can't all go. Somebody has to stay with the ship. Also, I need Tony for the survey. We're going to make a start this morning." He paused. "Now we know what we're looking for."

Duluth tossed up his bowl and caught it. He grinned, at Lukas. "You just been elected, Mike. Have a good time and don't get fresh with the women."

"Why don't you go yourself? I thought you would be straining at the leash, Joe. Something wrong?"

"No, nothing wrong," said Duluth innocently. "Only I'd like someone else to find out if these boys are cannibals. . . . Be a pal and bring back some more free samples. I got an idea Trans-Solar won't worry about a few kilograms—not where I put 'em."

Five minutes later Lukas was trailing across the sand belt

towards the forest, walking with the old hominid at the head of the column.

Alsdorf watched the procession silently for a while, then said, "Did he take a machine pistol?"

Chirico began to examine the curious pattern on his bowl. "He didn't take anything, Kurt. At least I don't think so."

"He must have the death wish," said Alsdorf genially. He turned to Duluth. "How about improving your muscle tone, Joe? There's a lot of gear to be stowed in the tractor."

The village proved to be a couple of dozen two-room huts with adobe walls and thatches woven of thin branches and fronds. It stood in a small clearing by a stream in the forest, about three kilometers from the *Henri Poincare*.

In his own way Lukas had previously tended to romanticize the "noble savage." In discussions with Alsdorf throughout the long star voyage he had based his arguments relating to the decadence of civilization on the assumption that primitive man had in him some heroic element—a crude innocence, perhaps—that had slowly been depraved by the development of synthetic power. By synthetic power he meant the output of all machinery whose energy did not derive directly from man himself. Because terrestrial humanity no longer lived by the sweat of its brow but had learned to rely upon steam, petroleum, atomic energy and solar power to take care of the donkey work, Lucas had felt that some vital indefinable force had been irrevocably lost. Secretly Lukas despised himself as the product of a machine culture. Secretly he despised the fascination space travel had for him, because it was the ultimate in reliance upon machines. As a child he had read stories, half legend, half fact, of the extinct races—the North American Indians, the Eskimos, the Polynesians. Their starkly primitive existence had enthralled him. Their eventual extinction—the work of modern man—had dealt a sharp blow to his early and conventional faith in the benefits of science. Ever since, he had regarded his own aptitude and affinity for machines with a mixture of guilt and hate. And though he turned out to be a first-class pilot, he both distrusted his skill and was ashamed of it. He was still unconsciously yearning for the simple life.

The village to which the hominids led him came as a small shock. It was squalid and it stank. He knew then that he had expected something better.

The women, as well as the men, were entirely naked. The

129

slack bellies, the pendulous breasts sagged wearily as they struggled with pitchers of water from the stream, or returned from the morning's forage with a basket of fruit and a couple of rickety children dancing at their heels. But the overwhelming atmosphere was one of lassitude, almost of exhaustion.

He took in the scene with a feeling that perhaps Alsdorf was right, after all. Perhaps Fomalhaut Three would benefit even by the commercially "civilizing" ventures of Trans-Solar Chemicals, and even if all the hominids were reduced to the status of coolies. At least Trans-Solar would give them medical aid, clean living conditions, and rectify any deficiency of vitamins.

The old hominid who had presented the platinum bowls and then offered his pathetic hospitality was called Masumo. He led Lukas into one of the adobe huts and invited him to squat on the sanded floor. Presently they were served bowls of vegetable milk and sliced yams by an old crone. Lukas stared at the refreshment distastefully but decided to risk it. After all, he supposed, it was possible even for an apelike creature in a jungle slum to feel insulted.

Surprisingly, Masumo's main interest lay in getting Lukas to talk—not the hominid tongue but his own language. By a complicated amalgam of signs, gestures and sounds, he indicated his wish for Lukas to talk of his own world, of cities and spaceways. It was some time before the general idea became apparent, and Lukas obliged only with reluctance, feeling that it was going to be like talking to a blank wall.

But after a while he began to warm up to his subject. He almost forgot Masumo's presence in the queer sensation that he was talking something out for himself. He described the vast metropolitan culture that had developed on Earth, the slow convergence of East and West, the origin of the federated world government after the first and last atomic war, the exploration of the solar planets, and the race for the stars.

And as he talked an obscure pattern seemed to be taking shape at the back of his mind.

It was nearly sunset by the time Lukas got back to the ship. Duluth was waiting for him, but the others were still out with the tractor.

"Hello, Mike. Been making whoopee with the village maidens? How did it go?"

Lukas told him.

The engineer stared at him incredulously. "Boy, one of us

130

has had sunstroke—and I'm feeling all right. You say you spent most of the time talking *English?"*

"That's what the old boy wanted." He scratched his head and frowned slightly. "Somehow it seemed perfectly natural once I got started. . . . You should see that village, Joe; it's an education. . . . Well, what have you been doing with yourself?"

Duluth grinned. "I played truant. Things were so damn quiet around here, I fixed up the monowheel and went for a run. Covered about a hundred kilometers, I guess."

"See anything of Kurt and Tony?"

"Nope. I went north. Funny thing, Mike, you'd think there'd be a hell of a lot of wild life about, wouldn't you?"

"So?"

"So there just isn't, that's all. When I'd done about fifteen kilometers I got fed up with the sand and went for a spin in the forest. Saw a few birds, squirrels and something that looked like a rabbit. But no big game. What do you make of that?"

"Nothing. What should I make of it?"

"I don't know. It just seems mighty peculiar. Come to think of it, this whole damn set-up is might peculiar—too stinking quiet."

Lukas suddenly remembered the peculiar feeling he had when Masumo presented him with the platinum bowl that morning. He was about to mention it to Duluth, but was distracted by a flashing pencil beam of light over toward the forest line. "Here they come," said Lukas. "Kurt has the headlights on."

A few minutes later Alsdorf and Chirico clambered up to the mess-deck. The geophysicist's eyes were gleaming with satisfaction.

"Palladium and platinum," he said, trying to keep the tremor out of his voice. "Concentrated alluvial deposits! You can fill your pocket with nuggets without taking a dozen steps. Here, take a look at these." He passed a few small irregular blackish stones for inspection.

"Looks to me like small slag," said Duluth, unimpressed.

"They're covered with iron oxide," explained Alsdorf impatiently. "There is more platinum to the square kilometers here than the entire output of the solar planets. We've made history. This thing is going to be so big—"

"I'll bet that fills the hominids with joy," said Lukas dryly.

Alsdorf laughed. "We found a few of their crude artifacts lying around. Fiber shovels and picks . . . Imagine it, they have platinum and palladium but they don't have iron." His laughter was uproarious.

Chirico stared at Lukas intently. "You look down in the mouth, Mike. Is something wrong?"

"Negative," said Lukas, with a faint smile.

Alsdorf collected his precious nuggets and put them back into his pocket. "How did the party go, Mike? Did they try to poison you?"

"Didn't need to. That village of theirs is one unholy stinkpot."

The German shrugged. "What did you expect? In a couple of years there won't be any village. We will introduce the hominids to the concept of organized effort. They don't know it yet, but they're going to build a spaceport."

Lukas gave a wry grin. "You think they'll be enthusiastic?"

"We'll convert them." Alsdorf was full of confidence, full of the civilized man's self-assurance, secure in the knowledge that—as so often before—machines and psychological warfare would make the domination of a tribe of savages no problem at all.

The following morning, after an early meal, Alsdorf and Chirico set out in the tractor to continue their survey. Duluth stayed in the ship doing a few small maintenance jobs. But by midday he had finished, and suggested that he and Lukas go for a spin in the monowheel.

"Not for me, Joe," said Lukas, staring moodily through a transparent panel on the navigation deck. "Among other things, I'm going to bring the log up to date. Haven't had time for it so far."

"Suit yourself," said Duluth. "I'm going to shoot me a squirrel if I can't find anything bigger. Maybe I'll take a look at shantytown on the way back."

He went down the companion ladder. Presently Lukas saw the monowheel hurtling along at high speed over the smooth sand belt. He watched till it became a small speck, then turned to the chart table and reached for the star log. He began to make concise entries in a neat, steady handwriting.

He had been working for about twenty minutes when a voice said softly in his ear: *"Masumo would speak with Lukas of the sky machine."*

Lukas jumped as if he'd been stung. He spun around, but there was no one else on deck. Then he looked through the observation panel and saw down below a small, naked figure in the distance. It was coming toward the *Henri Poincare*. Puzzled, Lukas went down to meet it.

"Did you talk to me while I was in the sky machine?" he asked abruptly.

But Masumo only smiled, raised his leathery arm in greeting and offered the traditional salutation in his own language. Lukas returned it and together they walked back to the ship.

Oddly enough, Lukas had already forgotten about the voice, and did not remember it until much later. Suddenly he wanted to show Masumo the interior of the ship, wanted to see his reaction to the wonders of terrestrial science.

He gestured toward the ladder. The hominid smiled and scrambled up it with incredible speed. Lukas followed and began the conducted tour.

If he expected a violent reaction—a display of superstition, dread or near-worship—he was disappointed. Masumo looked at volatility tubes, pile drives, Kirchhausen units, refrigerators, contour-berths, electronic cookers and motion-picture projectors with the same bland smile. It was as if, thought Lukas, the old hominid was on guard against something—too much on guard to remember that he ought to be suitably astounded.

Only once did Masumo forget himself. They were on the navigation deck and Lukas had just shown him the manual telescope, pointing it toward the forest line and letting him look through. But even the glass that made things magically near did not shake Masumo. He treated it with that same unwavering smile.

Baffled, Lukas turned his attention to the small transceiver, intending to make radio contact with the tractor and see if Masumo would react to voices that he would recognize. He tried five hundred kilocycles, the agreed frequency, and called repeatedly. But as there was no answer he concluded that Alsdorf and Chirico were out working on foot. As Lukas got up from the radio bench he suddenly saw Masumo staring with poorly repressed excitement at a star chart. He stood still and watched for a moment, noting the quick alert interest and the way Masumo swiftly moved his skinny finger from one constellation to another.

Then, aware that Lukas was staring at him, Masumo seemed to withdraw once more into his role of ignorant savage. The bland smile settled over his face like a mask.

"Masumo, you know what those are, don't you?" demanded Lukas, pointing to the star charts.

But the hominid affected not to understand and said in his

133

own tongue: "Talk to me, man of the sky. Talk to me of your voyage across the ocean of many suns."

Certain now that Masumo was practicing some elaborate deception, Lukas wanted to shake the truth out of him. Instead he found himself obeying the old hominid with a strange sense of emotional submission—as if his willpower had been paralyzed.

Masumo left the *Henri Poincare* a little before sunset—long enough to give him sufficient light to get back to the village. A few minutes after the hominid had gone Lukas managed to rouse himself from a mental and emotional stupor. He had the sensation of awakening from some peculiar dream. He lit a cigarette, poured himself a stiff drink and tried to consider the events of the afternoon calmly.

He was still puzzling the situation out when Duluth returned from his trip in the monowheel. The engineer found Lukas on the mess-deck, looking—as Duluth remarked—like a pile of ectoplasm left over from a phony seance.

"What's eating you, Mike? Somebody been making nasty faces through the window?"

Lukas pulled himself together and gave a laconic account of Masumo's visit. Duluth pursed his lips and let out a long, low whistle.

"I had a feeling those simple-minded characters were too good to be true," he said slowly. "I got something else for us to think about, as well. In case you haven't noticed it, they never talk to each other. They make plenty of gibberish for our benefit, but they don't use it among themselves. I looked in at shantytown to say hello on my way back this afternoon. I was there a couple of hours, maybe. There was plenty of noise, all right—and all of it directed at me. I thought there was something mighty fishy, but it didn't dawn on me what it was until I was heading back to the ship."

Lukas sat up suddenly. "Joe, you've hit it! These creatures have been taking us for a ride. They're natural telepaths."

Duluth shrugged. "If they're so goddam clever, why do they look like a gorilla's next of kin? Why do they live the way they do?"

"That's what we're going to find out."

At that moment they heard sounds down below indicating that Alsdorf and Chirico had returned with the tractor. Duluth went down to meet them. A few moments later Alsdorf hurried up the companion ladder. There was a curious, strained look on his face.

"Mike, what is your opinion of witchcraft?" he asked abruptly.

Lukas raised his eyebrows. "I haven't any. You'd better tell me the worst."

The German slumped onto a bench. His gaze fell on the newly opened bottle of whisky. He reached for it and took a deep drink—straight from the bottle. Lukas was intrigued. This was the first time he had ever seen Alsdorf lose his smooth sang-froid.

"Palladium and platinum deposits," said Alsdorf, coughing a little. "They've completely disappeared."

"What!"

The geophysicist nodded emphatically. "Not a trace. They might never have existed. Nothing disturbed, no sign of interference. But not a trace of nuggets, ore or any damn thing. . . . Acres and acres of it, Mike, and the whole lot wiped clean out of existence." The shock to his scientific soul was such that he seemed about to burst into tears.

Lukas stared at him. "But the thing is impossible. You're sure?"

Alsdorf slammed the bottle down. "Don't ask me if I'm sure it's the right place. Tony and I nearly went crazy making sure. . . . How could it happen, Mike? It's impossible!"

"It *was* impossible, you mean." Lukas stood up. "It looks as if this is our big day, doesn't it?" He gazed through the observation panel at the darkening sky over the forest line and began to tell Alsdorf about Masumo's visit.

By the time he had finished the geophysicist had regained control of himself. "Tonight," he said somberly, "we will make our plans. Tomorrow we will take the tractor and pay these hominids a visit—with machine pistols, grenades and gas bombs." He laughed mirthlessly. "The experiment will be conducted under scientific conditions. We will see if they are—vulnerable."

"Are you proposing to blast them to glory?" demanded Lukas quietly. "Because if so, you can think again. This is their planet, not ours."

Alsdorf gave him a sour grin. "Still the adolescent idealist, Mike. Why don't you grow up?"

"Don't worry, I am," retorted Lukas. "Meanwhile, don't think I'm going to let you intimidate a bunch of defenseless savages."

"I get the impression that they are not so defenseless nor so ignorant as we thought," remarked Alsdorf pleasantly.

135

"And while I have no intention of being dramatic I'm damn well going to find out what's happened to our platinum."

"Our platinum?" Lukas stared at him.

"Ours by right of conquest," amended Alsdorf dryly. "We have the superior culture, the superior tools and the superior weapons."

Lukas suddenly laughed. "But we aren't telepaths and we can't do vanishing tricks with large platinum deposits. Don't get overconfident, Kurt."

Chirico came up the companion ladder, preceded by a loud blast of invective.

"Those lousy, stinking aboriginals! Those sons of a venereal ape! Hi, Mike. I hear you have been having fun, too. . . . What beats me is how they could possibly—"

Duluth, who had followed him, said calmly, "I have a theory." The three men turned and stared at him.

Duluth helped himself to a cigarette and lit it. "Yeah," he said with an air of profundity, "they do it with mirrors."

After the evening meal a formal conference was held on the navigation deck. Alsdorf opened it by proposing to make a lightning swoop on the village to capture Masumo, with the logical aim of holding him as a hostage and finding out what he knew. Lukas, as captain of the ship, and therefore the person responsible for the safety of the expedition, promptly vetoed the proposal.

"Are you suggesting, Mike, that we do nothing, that we just hang around waiting to see what happens next?" Alsdorf was scathing.

"Keep your shirt on. Leaving aside the ethics of the thing, I'm merely pointing out that we can't afford to start anything unless we're sure we can finish it. If Masumo is a telepath we'd be fools to have him in the ship. It's possible he would be able to report on every move we made."

"Unfortunately," said Chirico with a wry smile, "Mike happens to be right. We do not know how these—these primitive poltergeists operate. . . . But, hell, we have to do *something,* don't we?"

"Why not get out of here and touch down somewhere else?" asked Duluth lazily. "Anything for a quiet life."

Alsdorf withered him with a glance. "And lose the finest platinum deposits we're ever likely to see?"

"Correct me if I'm wrong," drawled Duluth, "but haven't we already lost 'em?"

Glancing quickly from face to face Lukas could see that

the expedition's morale had reached a crucial phase. While he personally would gladly have accepted Duluth's suggestion, for some reason that he could not yet fully understand he realized that it was psychologically unsound. For the first time in history a space crew had come up against a quasi-human culture—one that was both beyond and below its terrestrial equivalent—and they could not, with self-respect, ignore its challenge. To do so would be to admit that their own sense of superiority was hollow. And Lukas was dimly aware that if human beings were to realize that they could be beaten by a different kind of creature, with a different concept of power, it would be as big a shock as the original discovery that Earth was not the fixed center of the universe.

He looked at the faces of his companions and offered the compromise he had decided upon at the beginning.

"Kurt would like to get tough with the hominids," he said slowly, "but we agree that we're not in a position to get tough. Joe suggests pulling up anchor and trying elsewhere. But that is no good, either. Sooner or later this kind of problem will occur again. We have to try and tackle it here. . . . I suggest that tomorrow three of us—with defensive arms, if it makes you feel better—take the tractor and pay them a visit, the aim being to try to find a peaceful solution. One thing we do know, the hominids will understand what we are getting at—if they want to understand. If they don't feel like cooperating over the platinum, well, we'll have to think again. . . . But this is their territory and we can't afford to create a situation that might jeopardize the next space crew to get here."

Chirico made up his mind immediately. "That's the best idea yet, Mike. If the hominids really are mindreaders they'll know we aren't out for trouble, and they might be willing to meet us. . . . What do you say, Kurt?"

The geophysicist shrugged. "I think they will laugh at us. But I'm willing to try diplomacy—once."

"It could be interesting," remarked Duluth. "I'm for it—provided I'm not elected to stay behind and guard the ship. If they can knock off the platinum deposits they might take it into their nuts to have a crack at vanishing the *Poincare*."

"That's my responsibility," said Lukas. "You three had better get some sleep, while I take the first watch."

It was late afternoon before the expedition started. Lukas had suggested the delay in case the hominids themselves chose to make a visit. But though a constant watch had been kept on the forest line no movement had been observed, and it looked as if the hominids were content to rest on their achievements so far.

Alsdorf's defensive armament consisted of two machine pistols and a box of gas bombs. He stowed himself, the gas bombs and one machine pistol in the tractor's observation turret, while Duluth took the other machine pistol below and sat with Chirico, who was the driver.

Lukas came down the ladder to see them off. He exchanged a few last-minute words with Alsdorf, who had decided to ride with the turret hatch open—in case quick action was needed.

"How is the adrenaline, Kurt?"

The geophysicist gave him a thin smile. "I'm not trigger-happy, if that's what you mean."

Lukas grinned. "If they start throwing telepathy at you, don't waste time with the sleep bombs. Get the hell out of there."

"We'll see."

Lukas went to the driver's compartment. "I'll call you on the transceiver in fifteen minutes, Joe. Don't let them pull any rabbits out of your hat."

Duluth laughed. "Maybe we'll use a little magic ourselves."

Chirico waved and switched on the engine. Presently the tractor was lumbering purposefully toward the forest in a dead straight line.

Lukas went back to the navigation deck and settled down to wait and watch. He lit a cigarette and made himself comfortable in the astrodome, thus commanding the view on all sides. There was nothing to be seen. Eventually he realized it was time for the radio check. He climbed down the short ladder and switched the transceiver on.

"Ship to tractor, ship to tractor. Have you made contact yet?"

"Tractor to ship." Lukas recognized Duluth's voice. "Tractor to ship. We hit shantytown a couple of minutes ago. Kurt is raising his blood pressure trying to make Masumo understand what he's talking about. The old son of an ape is playing stupid. Looks as if he's enjoying it, too. . . . Any development your end?"

"Dead quiet. I hope it stays that way. . . . I'll leave this set on receive, then you can call me any time."

"O.K. Mike. This is the picture so far. The old boy wanted to take Kurt into one of those adobe shacks—a bit bigger than the rest. It looks like some kind of council chamber. But Kurt wasn't having any. So he and Masumo are standing just in front of the tractor. The louder Kurt shouts, the more the old boy seems to like it. At the moment he's calmly drawing patterns in the sand with a pointed stick. You know, they look like star maps. . . . Jesus, they are star maps! Mike, can you believe this—he's plotted our course for a solar deceleration! Now Kurt has really lost his temper. Any moment now he'll start tossing something. . . . Hey, Kurt! For Chrissake—"

Suddenly Duluth's voice was cut off. Lukas felt the sweat forming on his forehead. Immediately he threw the switch to transmit.

"Ship to tractor! Joe! What's happened? Are you receiving me?"

There was no background noise—nothing.

Lukas stared dully at the transceiver, trying to work out all possibilities. Mechanical failure was possible, but least likely. Somebody or something had blasted the transmission.

Minutes went by and nothing happened. Lukas hauled himself up into the astrodome and gazed intently on all sides. The landscape was as empty as ever. He went down and tried the transceiver again but his calls were unanswered. He tried to decide what to do. But all the plans he devised were blocked by the basic fact that he must not leave the ship unguarded. That would be the final stupidity. Again he tried the transceiver, and again there was no response. He could only wait and hope.

Meanwhile the sun moved slowly down the yellowish sky until it hung over the forest. Mechanically Lukas swung himself up into the astrodome for the twentieth time and looked around. Then he saw something moving and grabbed the telescope.

He couldn't believe his eyes. The tractor was halfway across the sand belt, heading straight for the *Henri oPincare*. Sitting crosslegged in front of its turret, rocking gently with the tractor's motion and looking like a somnolent toad, was Masumo.

Lukas jumped down from the dome. Simultaneously he knew that everything had gone wrong, and yet somehow it was all right.

Then he heard a voice speak softly in his ear: *"Be not afraid, man of the skymachine. I come in peace."*

Against all reason—even against his will—Lukas laid down

139

the machine pistol he had just picked up, and felt the tension drain out of him. The words had reacted on him not as a command but as a compulsion. Calmly he went down the companion ladder and out of the spaceship. He stood on the still-warm sand, watching the tractor draw near.

It pulled up smoothly, and at the same time Masumo stood up, jumped lightly from the turret and raised his hand in the customary greeting. On his face was a fixed bland smile.

Lukas almost ignored him. His attention was riveted to the tractor.

Chirico was sitting at the wheel, stiff as a ramrod, gazing fixedly ahead with a vacancy of expression that seemed to suggest a state of hypnosis. Duluth, his eyes open, his brain still working, had slumped on his seat in a catatonic stupor. Alsdorf lay quietly on the floor, curled up in a tight fetal ball.

With a sudden blaze of anger Lukas turned to Masumo, raising his arm for a crushing blow. Then he saw the expression in the old hominid's eyes, and his arm dropped impotently to his side.

It was as if the landscape had darkened; as if Masumo had somehow become luminous; as if he had grown taller than the ship. As if his head had suddenly filled the yellow sky.

Lukas gazed at the eyes, fascinated. They became lakes, then whirlpools of infinite depth, drawing him down. Masumo's smile did not change, his lips did not move, but the voice spoke once more.

It was a calm, quiet voice. And yet, the voice of thunder.

"Man-of-the-sky, you came to my village and I read your heart. I saw there the picture of your machinemade civilization, its dreams of conquest, its nightmares of fear. Your people are but children. We can allow them to play a little longer. But presently they must put away their childish toys. Presently they must learn to take their place as a single world-spirit in the star culture of immortals.

Men live and die. But the racial purpose is beyond time. We of this world had learned to surrender to that purpose, to become one with all world-spirits throughout the vast pattern of stars, before your people could stand upright on two feet.

Some day your race will find itself and freely follow the universal destiny. We, the enlightened ones, whom you have chosen to see only as ignorant savages, will await you. Until then it is our task to see that you do not plunder the stars too much.

140

Suspecting the reason for your visit, Man-of-the-sky, we tested you and your companions with the rare metals you desire. And thus we learned how far you have yet to travel to reach enlightenment. . . .

You will leave this planet now. When you are voyaging through the dark oceans of the sky your companions will recover. But neither they nor you will remember these happenings. You will know only that the journey was futile, that the planet was barren of all your sought. . . . Farewell, Man-of-the-sky. May your people reach the ultimate tranquility in which diverse worlds—greater in number than the sands of the sea—have found their common end."

Suddenly Massumo seemed to return to his normal stature. He raised his arm once more to Lukas, lightly touched the center of his forehead, then turned and walked slowly away over the sand belt toward the dark line of the forest.

Lukas watched until the hominid was no more than a moving speck. Then, like a remotely controlled automata he went to the tractor.

Presently, some time after the sun had set, the *Henri Poincare* emitted a jet of green flame from its planetary drive. Swiftly it began to climb in a blinding arc until, moving up into the reaches of sunlight again, its path was etched like a bow of burning gold.

In the few seconds before it passed beyond the visible range it was observed from the surface of Fomalhaut Three— by eyes that were no longer dark and without luster. Eyes that radiated an incomprehensible power, that glowed like twin diamonds, that burned like bright, binary stars.

THE INTRUDERS

It was as if the universe had suddenly made up its mind to turn around. Slowly, impressively, shoals of pinpoint diamonds, floating through a sea of total darkness, began to swim in orderly rhythm round the moonship. Presently Earth swung like a Hallowe'en lantern across the starboard bow, and the moon itself came dead astern.

Six hours ago the moonship had crossed the neutral frontier in its long free fall through a quarter of a million miles of silence. Now, after five days of zero gravity, the time for action had arrived.

The stars stopped turning and the green Earth-lantern hung itself on some invisible hook. The universe was still once more: the moonship had swung into position for its stern-first landing.

Five hundred miles away, pitted lunar craters yawned menacingly at the falling ship. They expanded, displaying hidden contours, desolate rocky fangs, and all the nightmarish immobility of a petrified world.

Six anxious pairs of eyes gazed at the external visulators on the navigation deck. They saw the crater Tycho, surrounded by cracked and wrinkled lava-plains, rushing up as if eager to snatch the moonship clean out of existence.

In less than ten minutes, six men would have fulfilled a centuries-old dream of conquest, having reached the moon alive—or else there would be another smaller crater fifty miles from Tycho, a tiny cup of steam and heat and vaporized metal in the vastness of the lunar silence.

Captain Harper gazed hypnotically at the screen in front of his contour-berth and wondered whether it would do any good to pray. Professor Jantz, mathematician and astronomer, attempted to stave off an elemental fear by working out the cube of 789. Doctors Jackson and Holt, geologist and chemist, exchanged whispered instructions in the impossible possibility that either would survive the other. Pegram, the navigator, stroked a rabbit's paw; and Davis, the engineer, silently recited *The Golden Journey to Samarkand,* while clutching a battered photograph of the girl he might have married.

"Sixty seconds to firing point," boomed the auto-announcer. "Forty-five seconds . . . thirty seconds . . . fifteen seconds . . . ten, nine, eight, seven, six, five, four three, two, one—zero!"

A sudden surge of power slammed the men deep into the mattresses of their contour-berths. The port and starboard visulators showed a jet of yellow-green fire reaching down toward the moon from the stern of the ship.

After days of zero gravity the sudden G force developed a merciless pressure until it seemed as if human veins were filled with mercury, as if bone and tissue had been abruptly transmuted to lead.

On the visulator screen a long row of mountain fangs swept by, seeming to miss the ship's now extended spider-legs by inches. A smooth area of lavabed flashed into view, growing with terrifying speed until every detail, every fragment of rock, was sharply outlined.

142

Now the rocket motors were delivering maximum energy. There was no true sound aboard the moonship, but it seemed as if that tremendous liberation of chemical power had created a silent banshee moan that racked every girder, every metal plate, every human fiber with its high penetrating message.

Professor Jantz was no longer working out the cube of 789: he was unconscious. His companions, with varying degrees of discomfort, stared through mists of semi-consciousness at the bright pattern of images flashing on the bulkhead visulators.

The entire cosmos seemed to be pictured on the starboard, port and stern screens. The seconds ticked by, recorded by the thin red needle of the electrochron, hammering out their message like distant gunfire.

"Sixty seconds to zero altitude," boomed the auto-announcer.

Instinctively the men strained to look at each other, to exchange smiles of farewell or anticipatory grins of triumph.

"Forty-five seconds . . . thirty seconds . . . fifteen seconds . . . ten, nine, eight, seven, six, five, four, three, two, one—zero!"

There was silence—the loudest silence ever known. And stillness. Then relief.

As the three spider-legs contacted the lunar surface, the moonship's automatic pilot synchronized the fading of rocket motors with the vessel's fast-diminishing momentum. The spindly legs bit cautiously through an inch or two of liquid rock to be hard layer below. There was no bump, no sudden lurch, no sickening wobble. Only the end of something. The end of movement, of accelerating G forces, of flashing images on the visulator screens, of fear and discomfort . . . the end of a brief but colossal climax of stress.

Captain Harper was the first to find his voice. "Zero altitude," he said quietly. "Only the good die young!"

Professor Jantz opened his eyes; Pegram, the navigator, surreptitiously put away his rabbit's paw; and Davis stopped reciting The Golden Journey to himself. They began to undo their contour-berth straps and presently feeling the steady lazy tug of one-sixth gravity, everyone crowded up into the observation dome.

Twenty-four hours later the moonship stood like a three-legged skeleton with only the personnel sphere set perkily on top of its tubular backbone. At the base of this hundred-foot-high derelict that had completed its first and last journey through space, there lay a lunar tractor and trailer, a neat stack of curved metal plates, and a large number of crates of varying shapes and sizes.

The early sunlight cast long shadows in fantastic patterns behind all the goods and chattels of the advance expedition. Large and low in a jet black sky, the green ball of earth dominated its background of stars.

Meanwhile on the navigation deck in the personnel sphere Captain Harper was holding a final conference prior to abandoning ship.

"In four weeks, gentlemen," he was saying, "Number Two ship will arrive. Its cargo, as you know, will be mainly food and two more lunar tractors. If we can have the base well established by then, and if we manage to complete the preliminary survey, a great deal of time will be saved; and the equatorial expedition will be able to get straight off the mark. As there are only six of us, it's pretty obvious that we've got our work cut out. First thing, of course, is to get a living-unit fixed up. Until that's done there'll be no time for anything else. Dr. Jackson, you're the geologist; have you come across any likely niches where we can erect the unit safely?"

"I've found a perfect site," answered Jackson. "It's about a mile away, practically in a direct line with Tycho and the ship. There's a thirty-foot fissure with an overhanging shelf. It'll give perfect protection against meteorites. But we shall have to fix up a permanent staircase because the walls are damn near vertical all round."

"How many living-units will it contain?" asked Harper.

"At least three. I see no reason why it shouldn't house three units and the laboratory. And if, eventually, they decide to increase the expedition, there are several nearby crevices where one or two extra units could be placed."

"Dr. Holt, you explored the place with Jackson. What's your verdict?" The captain looked inquiringly at the chemist, who, being only thirty, was the youngest member of the party.

"There are plenty of ratholes around," said Holt, "but none of 'em quite so convenient. I agree with Jackson. We could do a lot worse."

"We'd better load up, then," said Captain Harper, reaching for the headpiece of his pressure suit. "The sooner we get the first unit erected, the better." He gazed through a plasti-glass porthole. "Something tells me we're going to get

144

thoroughly fed up with this dead landscape before we're through. . . . Any questions?"

"It's time to make a radio check with Earth," said Pegram. "Do you want to send a message, sir?"

Captain Harper lifted the headpiece and smoothed back his thick gray hair. "Tell them," he said humorlessly, "that this place is so dead, if we saw a blade of grass we'd probably scream."

It took three more terrestrial days to set up the living-unit in the fissure that Dr. Jackson had selected—by which time the sun had risen clear of the distant mountain ranges and hung like a blinding fireball in the black, star-pricked sky.

The lunar day, in length a terrestrial fortnight, had now reached the high flush of mid-morning.

While they were erecting the first living-unit Captain Harper and his companions ate and slept in the pressurized tractor, which was large enough to accommodate the six of them comfortably. Later, when it was used for long-distance reconnaissance work, they would have to live in it for over a week at a time. This first experience of life in its compact quarters was valuable training.

Now and again, between the endless tasks of hauling and erecting, the men would take a few minutes off just to stand and gaze and marvel at the hard, lifeless landscape under its roof of darkness.

They would become thunderstruck at their own smallness, at their colossal achievement, and at the notion that they themselves were probably the first organic lifeform ever to be established on the moon.

Fifty miles away, toward the lunar south pole, the crater Tycho displayed its sharp mountain ring with perfect clarity —teethlike over the faintly curved horizon. There were no atmospheric mists to soften its contours or take the edge of fire from its sunlit peaks.

Stretching away into the distance on every side of the fissure where Base One had been erected, the lava plains were covered with a two-inch layer of meteoric dust that fell as rapidly as it was disturbed, and retained footprints like new snow. When the lunar tractor swayed by in eerie silence, the dust was plowed back to leave a caterpillar-indented road. There was not much danger of wandering away from base and getting lost on the moon when footprints left a trail that, unless disturbed, would remain clear for thousands of years.

By the fourth terrestrial day the expedition was established in its subterranean living-unit. Most of the routine fetch-and-carry work was over. Now the real business of experiment and exploration could begin.

It was decided that Doctors Jackson and Holt, with Davis the engineer, should take the tractor and make a survey of a ten-mile radius, keeping radio contact. They were to return in six hours.

Captain Harper would have joined them but conscience kept him tied down to a pile of routine work at base. And Professor Jantz, having sampled the lunar dust, was completely absorbed in calculations relating to meteoric bombardment. Pegram, the remaining member of the expedition, had his own work to do. Apart from maintaining radio contact with Earth, he would also keep in touch with the tractor.

After a restless three-hour duty sleep, Jackson, Holt and Davis went into the dining room at Base One and ate a hearty breakfast.

Professor Jantz, with a finger-calculator on one side of his plate and a reference book on the other, peered at them through blue-tinted glasses.

"I want small crystals," he said abruptly, "and anything metallic. Look out for me, Jackson, there's a good fellow."

Jackson swallowed a mouthful of coffee and laughed. "What do you think *I* want, Professor? If there's anything worth having, we'll bring it back."

The professor nodded, then demanded with seeming irrelevance: "Why is there no oxygen on the moon?"

Dr. Holt put down his fork and gazed at the mathematician curiously. "You are aware of the conventional reasons, Professor?"

"Naturally—but they are not good enough."

"What makes you think that?"

Professor Jantz treated the younger man to a secretive smile. "My calculations," he said happily. "We are all going to be surprised."

"Bet you a double ration of brandy," said Dr. Jackson, "that there is definitely no trace of oxygen in any form."

Professor Jantz was silent for a moment. Then he said, "I am not only prepared to take your bet, Dr. Jackson, I am prepared to make an additional wager. I prophesy that we shall discover signs of organic matter."

"A week's tobacco says we won't."

"Good. I am a heavy smoker." The professor's confidence was such that he gave the impression of already having actual confirmation.

"Since you are so dogmatic," said Dr. Holt thoughtfully, "you might help us to prove your point by suggesting the type we must look for."

"It will have been sleeping for millions of years," said the professor. "We shall find it in caves or chasms but not, I think, near the main craters."

"Stop being enigmatic," said Jackson. "What the devil are you getting at?"

"Coal," said the professor impressively. "Beautiful carboniferous coal."

"Nuts!" retorted Jackson.

"Nuts and dust," said Jantz calmly, returning to his calculations.

They had been away from base about twenty minutes. Davis was driving and the tractor was making a steady twelve miles an hour. Dr. Jackson sat by his side in the pressurized compartment with a sketch pad strapped to his knee. Every now and then he made a few key notes or a diagram, and when he was not doing that he talked to Pegram, back at base, over the radio.

Dr. Holt was outside the tractor, squatting in the "crow's-nest" with a cine-camera. His only means of contact with the two occupants was his personal radio. The sun beat mercilessly down on his pressure suit and headpiece, but as yet the insulation was doing a good job and he felt reasonably comfortable.

"Hello, Base One. Hello, Base One," said Jackson. "We are four miles south of you, heading roughly toward Tycho. The going is comparatively smooth and the tractor handles well. Tell Professor Jantz that the dust layer gets deeper in some of the ruts and bubble holes. Very slight evidence of a tendency to drift. Over to you."

"Hello, tractor. Hello, tractor. Professor Jantz has fixed up the seismograph. He requests an explosion when you are about ten miles away. Please inform us before detonation. Over to you."

"Hello, Base One. We consider it a privilege to create the first synthetic moonquake. Will let you know when we are ready. Over to you."

"Personally," said Davis, "I couldn't care less. The only thing that would surprise me is if something moved."

Suddenly Holt's voice came urgently over the personal radio. "Stop the tractor and come out quick!"

Davis depressed the clutch and slipped into neutral. The motor gave a whine of relief.

"What is it?" called Jackson.

"Come out here and tell me," came the enigmatic reply. Holt had already clambered out of the crow's-nest and was walking away from the tractor, peering carefully at the ground.

Davis and Jackson reached for their headpieces, screwed them down, tested oxygen and radio, then went into the airlock. A few moments later they joined Holt.

"What do you make of this?" asked Holt with suppressed excitement. He pointed down at the dust layer.

"Well, I'll be damned!" said Jackson. "Man Friday himself!"

He was staring at a set of clear footprints in the telltale lunar dust. Impulsively he planted his own foot down by one of the strange prints and compared the size. His own was narrower and four inches shorter.

"Now," said Holt, "follow the line."

Jackson let his gaze run along the trail until it disappeared in the distance. There were two sets of prints: one coming and one going. They ran in dead straight parallel lines toward the crater Tycho.

"What do we do?" asked Davis. "Radio to base?"

"Don't be in such a hurry," said Jackson irritably. "The good Lord placed an ornamental bulge on the end of your neck. Try to use it."

"I'm going to give it thirty seconds of film," announced Holt, unslinging his cine-camera. "Looks like Professor Jantz was being a little conservative when he hit on coal as the only evidence of organic life."

"Something has walked from the direction of Tycho," said Jackson half to himself. "It came and apparently stood here a bit, then turned around and walked back. Now why should it do that? It must have had a purpose."

"Exercise," suggested Holt flippantly. "The lunarian idea of a constitutional."

"I'm not in the mood for schoolboy humor," said Jackson. "Think up something useful to say, or use less oxygen."

Davis suddenly pointed behind them. "Do you see what I see?" he asked.

They turned around and followed his gaze. Four miles away the stripped hulk of the moonship, with its personnel sphere catching the sunlight, was clearly visible—like a low-hung star.

"Holy smoke!" said Holt. "A shy welcome committee! He, she or it must have watched us touch down."

"What shall we do?" asked Davis. "Follow the tracks?"

"I don't think so," said Jackson slowly. "This is something the bright boys didn't bargain for. I think we'd better hot-foot it back to base and have a powwow."

"It wouldn't do any harm to follow the tracks for a little way," suggested Holt.

"What for?"

"You never know, we might pick up some more evidence that will give us a better idea of the character who made them."

"Also," sead Jackson dryly, "we might bump into the aforementioned character. And he might invite us home for coffee and cream cakes. On the other hand, he might not approve of—intruders."

Captain Harper gazed at the faces of his five companions. "Well, we have heard Dr. Jackson's story and seen the film of the tracks. We now have to consider what we are going to do about the situation. As you know, nothing like this was envisaged when we left Earth. Any suggestions?"

Professor Jantz stroked his jaw thoughtfully. "The track marks indicate a biped of considerable stature. There is no appreciable atmosphere on the moon, therefore the creature can do without it, or else he provides his own. It would be safe, I think, to assume that he provides his own. This scems to presuppose a somewhat complex or decidedly intelligent being. The point is, would we be correct in assuming that there are many of his kind?"

"The point is, are we going to investigate?" said Dr. Holt. "Or are we going to try to avoid it or them until the next moonship arrives?"

"It or they may decide to investigate us," observed Captain Harper. "The main problem is, will they be dangerous and will they be hostile? I pleaded with the Organization Group to let me have some offensive weapons on this trip. But they carefully pointed out that no life could exist here. Silly bastards! They gave me a string of figures showing how many tons of fuel it would take to lift a u/s vibrator unit. And now the whole project may be in danger because some blasted animal doesn't subscribe to their cockeyed little theories."

"Don't worry about weapons, Captain," said Holt. "The lab is operating now. In twelve hours I can dream up some rocket grenades that'll take care of considerable opposition."

"Also," said Dr. Jackson, "we have enough high explosive to lay a minefield, to be detonated either by contact or radio."

Captain Harper drummed the edge of the table with his fingers for a few moments before replying. "In any case," he said finally, "we must have something with which to protect ourselves. My own opinion is that we must postpone action for a few hours until we have a supply of hand and rocket grenades and, perhaps, radio mines."

"Then what?" asked Dr. Holt.

"Then, I think, we must send a party to follow the tracks. It is imperative that we discover whether—whether there is any danger. Apart from our own safety, there is the rest of the expedition to consider."

"When the products of two culture patterns meet," remarked Jantz thoughtfully, "there is an inevitable conflict. I wonder which will triumph?"

There was a brief silence.

"The moon is barren," said Holt irrelevantly. "Now what could friend X possibly have for breakfast?"

Captain Harper decided to go on the reconnaissance himself, taking Jackson and Davis with him. Holt would remain behind, making more grenades and a few radio-controlled land mines. Professor Jantz and Pegram would alternately patrol on the surface and handle radio communications.

A double track in the luner dust had entirely disrupted the plans of the advance expedition. They had already begun to feel as if they were in a state of siege. It would not have been so bad if the tracks had been those of a four-footed creature. But a biped suggested power and high evolutionary development. If it was indigenous to the moon there was no reason why it should not be present in great numbers. And if that was the case it would probably resent the intruders from space, just as earthlings would if the situation were reversed.

Harper and his companions took their load of food, water and grenades through the airlock of their underground base. They climbed up the metal staircase and went out into the blinding sunlight.

The supplies were dumped in the tractor and everything was checked prior to departure. Davis again took the driver's seat and while he started the motor Dr. Jackson established radio contact with the tiny metal world that was secreted in its deep fissure. Meanwhile, Captain Harper, with four hand grenades, took himself up to the crow's-nest, directly over the driver's seat.

"Tractor to base," said Jackson. "We are on our way. Will make routine checks every quarter of an hour. Over."

"Base to tractor," replied Pegram. "Receiving you loud and clear. Good hunting. Over and out."

The whine of the motor increased and the tractor began to lurch slowly over the dead lunar plains, following its own previous path.

After half an hour the place where Holt had first seen the alien footprints was reached without incident. This time progress had been more cautious. At one point Captain Harper, keeping a constant watch on the crater Tycho, which lay on the port side, thought he saw movement in the distance. But he eventually put it down to imagination and the fatigue engendered by staring across the bright, arid lava-plains. There was nothing—nothing but a silent wilderness. He began to think that the whole thing was some kind of illusion, until he suddenly caught sight of the tracks. They were so alarmingly distinct that they might have been created only five minutes before.

By common consent the three men left the tractor and took a close look at the almost mathematically spaced indentations.

"Man Friday has a very precise stride, hasn't he?" said Jackson. "I wonder how far *we* could walk in a dead straight line, keeping our footsteps evenly spaced."

"He's a big devil," said Harper. "There's damn near a yard and a half between prints. Well, let's get on his tail. The sooner we clear up this mystery and find out just what we're up against, the better I'll like it."

"It may not be very funny if he's collected a few play-mates to sit up and wait for us," said Jackson quietly.

"We've got to take the risk. We can't just sit down at base and wait till he leaves a visiting card. Can you get the tractor to do twenty-five, Davis?"

"Yes, sir. Provided we don't have to keep it up for more than fifty miles or so."

Captain Harper pointed to Tycho. "We won't. By the time we get there—if we get there—we'll all need a break."

"Why don't you have a spell inside, Captain? I'll take a watch in the crow's-nest."

Harper grunted his approval of Jackson's suggestion and the three men walked back to the vehicle. Presently it was lurching along the trail at twenty-five miles an hour.

151

They stopped the tractor about eight hundred yards away and Jackson came down from the crow's-nest for a hasty consultation. Directly ahead lay the one symmetrical feature in the whole irregular landscape. It was a smooth hemisphere, surfaced apparently with metal, lying flush against the lava-beds about five miles from the foothills of Tycho. It rose abruptly from the drab landscape like a giant ostrich egg half buried in sand. It seemed about forty feet high.

"Looks like we've found Man Friday's lair," said Jackson. "He must be a clever boy to fix up a nice metal hideaway. Wonder if it's pressurized?"

Captain Harper stared somberly through the thick glass of the tractor's observation dome. "The more I see, the less I like it," he announced slowly. "We now have concrete evidence that our friend is pretty civilized, if not scientific. I wonder what other pleasant surprises there are in store?"

Jackson remained silent.

"What's the plan of campaign, sir?" asked Davis. "Do we push on and investigate?"

"We've got to do something about it," said Harper. "We can't just pack up now and turn back. I suggest we approach slowly until we're a couple of hundred yards away. Then . . ." He hesitated.

"Then what?" asked Jackson.

"Then one of us will go forward alone to investigate—taking grenades, of course. The others will remain in the tractor to await developments."

"I'll go," said Davis suddenly.

"No," said Jackson. "This is my job. If Man Friday and his friends prove hostile, engineers become more important than geologists. I'm damn sure *I* couldn't fix the tractor if we had a breakdown—and the tractor might make all the difference. Don't you agree, Captain Harper?"

"Unfortunately, yes. But let's hope there won't be any melodrama. Now we'd better start."

The tractor crawled slowly forward until it was two hundred yards from the metal hemisphere. Then it stopped. Without wasting any time Dr. Jackson climbed down from the crow's-nest and walked ahead, with a grenade ready in each hand.

The smooth wall of the hemisphere was broken only by an open doorway. As he advanced Dr. Jackson could see a red glow inside. When he was ten yards away he stopped, peered through the plastiglass visor of his headpiece uncertainly, then covered the remaining distance in one quick bound. The two men in the tractor watched him disappear into the darkness.

Immediately Captain Harper spoke over the personal radio: "What's the set-up? Are you all right?"

With a sigh of relief he heard Jackson's voice loud and steady. "No one at home. Come and have a look. I'm beginning to believe in fairies!"

"What have you found?"

"It's either a technician's nightmare or some kind of laboratory. Hellfire! I'll believe anything now!"

"What's happened?" asked Harper urgently.

"I've just discovered what look like three king-size coffins!"

Three hours later the tractor had returned to base and Captain Harper was giving an account of the trip to Professor Jantz, Pegram and Dr. Holt, while Davis and Dr. Jackson kept watch on the surface. In view of the knowledge recently acquired it was felt now that two men should always be on surface patrol.

"The place wasn't at all pressurized," said Harper, "which is fairly significant. Its walls were about three inches thick with, I should guess, cavity or insulation layer. The dull red glow came from some sort of activated crystal suspended over a circular bench about five feet high that ran all around. There were various mechanical gadgets strewn all over the bench and some fairly large apparatus about which we just didn't have a clue. Jackson thought there was some geological equipment, and Davis swears that a sizable box of tricks underneath the bench was a radio transmitter. But not having seen junk like that before we could only guess vaguely at its functions."

"About these boxes you dramatically describe as coffins," said Professor Jantz. "Can you give me any more details?"

"They were ten feet long and lay horizontally. The hinged lids were open and we took a good look inside. They were made of black metal and lined with a sort of glassy fabric. When Dr. Jackson moved to touch it a spark shot across to his pressure suit and was grounded automatically. He didn't try again. They appear to have been occupied."

"This is damn funny," said Dr. Holt with a nervous laugh. "We thought the moon was uninhabited and now we've collected a trio of scientific zombies for next-door neighbors."

"I'm not laughing," said Harper bitterly. "At the moment my sense of humor is conspicuous by its absence. What happens if these creatures don't want to be friendly—if and when we meet 'em? They aren't going to use bows and arrows."

"The possible occupation of the—er—coffins presents an interesting train of thought," said Jantz enigmatically. "I begin to form a mental picture of an intelligent, muscular biped, about nine feet tall, who supplies his own atmosphere, conducts scientific experiments, ignores animal comfort and is capable of walking nearly a hundred miles in high temperatures."

"A pretty unpleasant sort of enemy," commented Harper.

"If he turns out to be an enemy," added Dr. Holt.

"Were there many tracks around the place?" asked the professor.

"Dozens."

"Did you follow any of them up?"

"We thought we'd better get back with the information so far acquired before we ran into trouble. Are you implying that we ought to establish contact?"

"As soon as possible," said Jantz. "At the moment we are afraid of them—yet we haven't seen them—and they, I presume, will be afraid of us. An unsatisfactory situation. We must do something to allay or confirm our fears so that we can plan a definite course of action."

"I've cooked up enough radio mines to lay a fairly close field around the base," said Holt. "We can make sure that this place is reasonably safe, anyway."

Suddenly the table shuddered and an empty coffee cup fell over. From years of experience the men instinctively listened for the sounds of the accompanying explosion. There was nothing.

"What the devil's that?" snapped Harper.

Pegram dashed to the transmitter. "Hello, surface patrol! What's happening? Over."

There was no answer. As he tried again Captain Harper and Dr. Holt put their headpieces on and hurried to the airlock.

"Hello, surface patrol. Hello, surface patrol. What is happening? Over."

After a few moments Jackson's voice came faintly: "For God's sake come quickly! The moonship is—is destroyed. I've got a leak in my pressure suit. . . ."

In three minutes Captain Harper and Dr. Holt had

154

reached the surface. For a moment they stood paralyzed, gazing at the tangled ruin of the moonship a mile away. Then they dashed to the lunar tractor, jumped aboard and headed for the wreckage at full speed.

They had gone three-quarters of the way when they came across Jackson. He was lying quite still on the hard rock. Dr. Holt jumped out of the tractor, lifted him bodily and brought him back into the pressurized compartment.

"Is he alive?" demanded Harper tersely as he started the motor.

"I think so. It's a very slow leak and he had the sense to turn the oxygen to full pressure." He began to unscrew Jackson's headpiece.

The geologist's lips quivered. He gave a tremendous shudder and opened his eyes. "Get Davis," he mumbled weakly. "He was only about fifty yards from the moonship."

"What did it?" asked Harper, keeping his eyes on the lava-plains ahead as he steered directly for the wrecked ship.

In normal atmospheric pressure Dr. Jackson was recovering quickly. The color returned to his face and he managed to sit up. "I didn't see a thing," he said with an effort. "The ship just crumpled. Then the shock wave dropped me on a sharp rock and I knew a leak had started. It was all I could do to switch oxygen and helium to full and pray you'd pick me up before the pressure dropped too much."

"Look, there he is!" exclaimed Holt. He pointed to a prone figure sixty yards away. As the tractor slid toward it the three occupants could see that Davis had no headpiece. But it was not till the tractor had stopped that they discovered that he also had no head.

"Poor devil," said Harper. "Too near the blast."

"He wouldn't even have time to feel it," said Dr. Holt in a subdued voice.

"God Almighty! Look at the mess!" exclaimed Harper. He pointed to the wreck.

The moonship had been destroyed most efficiently. The long spider legs and tubular backbone were twisted like tinfoil. The personnel sphere was nonexistent, but beads of molten metal, scattered like raindrops, gave ample testament of its utter destruction. No ordinary high explosives would have produced such tremendous heat. It could only have been achieved—by earthlings, anyway—with the use of atomic power.

Dr. Jackson was the first to break the silence. "I wonder," he said quietly, "if Man Friday is still hanging about?"

"There's not much cover here for a character nine feet high," said Holt. "Nor for his transport, if he has any."

Captain Harper started the motor again. "Better see if we can find any tracks," he said.

The tractor began to crawl slowly around the wreck in expanding circles.

The council of war, held in the pressurized living-unit below the lunar surface, was brief and to the point. The five men sat around the table, smoking and drinking coffee in quantities well above the legitimate ration.

"Well, we've had the reply from Earth," announced Harper grimly. "They're very sorry for us but they aren't going to send any more moonships until they know what we're up against."

"I'll bet they're already planning a nice epitaph," said Holt cynically.

"It was the logical answer," remarked Jackson. "What's the point of endangering the whole expedition?"

"The ethical problem can be left till later," observed Professor Jantz with a faint smile. "The most important thing at the moment is to decide what we are going to do."

"Return the compliment," suggested Holt. "We ought to go along to their hideaway and blast it to pieces. It may serve to warn them off for a while, and it may also stop them from presenting us with another atomic shell."

"If it was atomic," said Professor Jantz.

"It certainly wasn't H.E.," returned Jackson. "The personnel sphere was half vaporized."

"I think we are, at the moment, a little too belligerent," said the professor mildly. "After all, if our absent friends have been on the moon some time they have a right to resent intruders. Provided we remain hidden and inactive, there is no reason why they should not assume that they have already destroyed us."

"We followed their tracks," retorted Harper. "Obviously they'll follow ours. For all we know, they might be preparing to drop another atomic shell right here. In view of the fact that they have won the first round I think it's up to us to make sure they don't win the next. Besides, one of our party is already dead, and Dr. Jackson only survived by about ninety seconds. The longer we stay inactive, the more chance these creatures have of picking us off."

"I think Captain Harper is right," said Jackson. "We've

156

got to do everything we can either to destroy them or discourage them."

"We'll put it to a vote," said the captain. "Make a noise if you're in favor of having an all-out effort to make them lose interest."

There was an immediate response. Only Professor Jantz remained silent.

A couple of hours later preparations were complete. A radio-controlled mine field had been placed around the entrance to the base unit; practice throws had been made with dummy grenades, and the men had been gratified to discover that the moon's weak gravity enabled them to hurl a grenade with reasonable accuracy over two hundred yards. The improvised rocket bombard could deliver fifty pounds of high explosive at targets more than a mile away.

Captain Harper's strategy was extremely simple; it had to be, for their resources were severely limited. The rocket bombard would be mounted in the crow's-nest of the tractor, then three men would take the tractor on its destructive mission while the other two stayed at base.

If the tractor failed to return from its fifty-mile journey to the metal hemisphere near the foothills of Tycho, it would be the duty of the survivors to radio as much information as possible to Earth, while remaining hidden.

Pegram and Professor Jantz would stay at base while the others did what they could.

Each of the five men realized with bitter clarity that the fate of man's first expedition to the moon hung precariously in the balance. If they failed now another attempt might not be made for several decades.

Presently all the weapons and supplies were aboard the lunar tractor and everything was ready for departure. The three men piled aboard while Pegram and Jantz stood by, offering occasional suggestions and checking that nothing had been left behind.

"As from now," said Captain Harper over his personal radio, "we won't break radio silence unless it's a matter of life and death. Our friends may have some sort of direction-finding apparatus, and there's no point in making it easy for them."

"As a scientist I disapprove of your purpose," said Professor Jantz with irony. "But as a man—well, good luck, you people. I hope you succeed."

"It'll be just too bad if we don't," said Harper grimly.

Holt gave a dry laugh. "Tell them," he said, "that my

last thoughts were of mother."

"We're fighting for the human race," remarked Dr. Jackson. "Oh how we hate its bloody face."

Amid laughter that gave a brittle impression of being light-hearted, Captain Harper started the tractor, coaxed it into gear and let out the clutch. Leaving behind it a quick-falling wake of lunar dust, the tractor rocked silently across the blinding lava plains.

It was the expedition's sixth terrestrial day on the moon, but already it seemed as if they had never known any other existence. The earth itself had become an illusion, a receding dream. The only realities now were the hard, dusty lava plains, the distant craters, and the ominous power of unseen creatures—the threat of those elusive and apparently tireless beings whom Jantz sarcastically referred to as "our absent friends."

Pegram and the professor watched the tractor shrink until it was no more than a tiny beetle toiling over a rippling sea of rock.

From a black, star-studded sky, the sun flung down its harsh, unfiltered radiation, creating the unbelievable surface heat of a late lunar morning.

In the distance the mountains of Tycho rose grim and forbidding, bathed by the burning sunlight. The whole landscape, locked in its own peculiar stillness, looked like a painted desert—the backcloth of a drama of suspense and danger, as indeed it was.

Captain Harper stopped the tractor a mile away from the metal hemisphere, and after hasty confirmation of the general plan of attack Holt and Jackson got out. Holt took up position two hundred yards away on the left flank, and Jackson two hundred yards away on the right, thus preventing a direct hit knocking out the entire attacking force.

Armed with grenades, the two men would advance steadily until they were in throwing range, or encountered opposition. If they were able to demolish the building without tackling the enemy, they would do so and withdraw; if not, they would do their best to engage the defense while Captain Harper drove the tractor in as close as possible and used the rocket bombard.

As soon as they had reached their flanking positions Harper waved his arm in the observation turret, and the two men moved forward at an ungainly, bounding trot.

They were within four hundred yards of the hemisphere

before there was any sign of activity. Then suddenly a large shape, oddly human, appeared momentarily in the doorway of the strange building. It hesitated, disappeared again, reappeared almost instantaneously and began running toward Holt at a tremendous speed.

As it came clear into the sunlight the three men saw that it was completely encased by metal. Its arms, legs and thick-jointed body flashed dully as the strange being rapidly advanced.

Although it was nine feet high and uncannily human in shape, the human beings who now confronted it saw with a sudden shock that the outline between its shoulders was smooth and flat. The creature had no head.

Holt's arm jerked sharply and a grenade flashed toward his macabre adversary, who was now only a hundred and fifty yards away. The monster continued on his course without any attempt at evasion.

The explosion made no sound, but a dull shock wave carried even to the tractor, now four hundred yards to the rear.

The grenade had been aimed well, in spite of the monster's speed. It dropped about ten yards behind him. The blast would have torn a human being to bits, but that metal-covered body merely sailed through the void another half dozen yards, picked itself up and continued its rapid advance. Holt lifted his arm to hurl another grenade but he was too late. Something glittered in the monster's hand. For a split second a thin pencil beam of intense radiance flashed on.

With involuntary cries of horror, Jackson and Captain Harper saw Holt fall in a heap. Even at that distance it was easy to see that his body had been cut clean in two.

Instantly the creature, seeing one enemy destroyed, turned toward Jackson. For a moment it was still—a perfect target—and Jackson did not waste the opportunity. Two grenades in rapid succession flew toward their target even as the strange being ran to attack. Realizing intuitively that the creature would run straight at him, Jackson purposely let one of the grenades fall short.

Leaving the first grenade well behind, the monster ran full into the second explosion. For a moment it seemed to hang suspended—a tableau of complete surprise—then arms and legs and body hurtled up into the void, and fell separately.

Wasting no time inspecting the damage, Dr. Jackson turned immediately toward the metal hemisphere. Two more headless monsters had appeared. They seemed to be setting up some sort of apparatus.

Meanwhile Captain Harper slammed the tractor into top speed and drove crazily toward the target. Less than three hundred yards away he stopped suddenly, and having depressurized the tractor, went straight through the airlock, knocking his headpiece heavily against the hiduminium door.

One well-timed leap brought him up into the crows-nest beside the rocket bombard. Hastily aligning the rough sights, he pressed the detonator button.

His aim was too high. Fifty pounds of high explosive sailed harmlessly over the objective. But even as he feverishly reloaded he saw Jackson moving forward out of the corner of his eye.

The geologist ran quickly to within throwing range, hurled two more grenades and fell flat on his face. The first one didn't explode, but it would have made no difference, since it was about thirty yards short. The second, however, fell only eight or nine yards away from the two beings. Even as one of them raised the strange glittering weapon in his hand, the grenade exploded, blowing him and his companion over backward and flattening their apparatus.

Far from being mortally wounded, the two creatures picked themselves up with astonishing speed. One of them ran for his hand weapon, lying on the lava bed a few yards away; while the other quickly tried to reconstruct his small tripod and its ominous-looking cylinder.

But by this time Harper had not only reloaded, but had forced himself by supreme act of will to take slow and measured aim—realizing, perhaps, that the issue depended entirely on his next shot.

The heavy rocket grenade sped straight toward the hemisphere. For a terrible moment it seemed as if the charge would not detonate. Then there was a silent flash, and the lunar tractor shuddered violently. The sudden cloud of dust fell almost as rapidly as it had risen.

When it cleared, Captain Harper saw that the metal hemisphere and its strange occupants were utterly destroyed. All that remained was a jagged, smoking debris of twisted metal.

For a moment the two survivors remained perfectly still. Then Dr. Jackson picked himself up and began to walk unsteadily toward what had once been Dr. Holt. With slow, jerky movements Captain Harper climbed down from the rocket bombard and made as if to join him. Suddenly he collapsed. Dr. Jackson turned and ran to him.

"I—think it's a—slow leak," gasped Harper over his

160

personal radio. "Pressurize tractor—for God's sake!"

Jackson picked him up and staggered to the tractor. He pushed Harper through the airlock, climbed in himself, slammed the sealing door and turned on the air cylinders to full.

The leak must have been infinitesimal, for the captain recovered almost immediately.

"Thanks," he said shakily. "It's a bloody awful feeling, isn't it?"

"They haven't yet invented the words to describe it," remarked Jackson grimly. "You'll have to stay in the tractor till we get back."

"Blast! We ought to do something about Holt, but my brain isn't working clearly. Any suggestions?"

"None worth having. . . . You saw what happened?"

Harper nodded. "Our headless friend gave him something that makes h/v bullets seem like baby's toys. We ought to take a look at him, though."

"Would that be wise?" asked Jackson slowly.

"You mean because of radioactivity?"

"Among other things."

"What about the remains of their outpost, then? I'll drive the tractor in close. I shouldn't think the H.E. will have left anything in a sufficiently dangerous concentration. What do you think?"

"It's worth the risk. We might learn something useful about them."

Harper started the tractor and let it move slowly forward toward the area of devastation. He switched off the motor about twenty yards from the wreckage.

"You know something?" said Jackson, as he prepared to go through the airlock. "In a way, we're lucky. This is the second little bit of history we've been privileged to make."

"How do you mean?"

"That character who dropped Holt and charged at me," said Jackson, "was quite peculiar. I was nearer to him than you were. I saw him fall apart."

"What are you getting at?"

"Only that he wasn't made of frogs and snails and puppy dogs' tails," replied Jackson with irony. "You know, Captain, I think we must be the first human beings to do battle with a bunch of lethal robots. The fact that we took those three apart is quite significant, really."

"Good God!" exclaimed Harper.

Dr. Jackson turned and went through the airlock. Presently

he was poking about among the glaring sunlit wreckage.

The crisis was over, but at Base One it took some time for the atmosphere of high tension to die down. Two men of the first expedition had died and the whole moon project had been on the edge of failure. Only a slow and intensive search of the entire base area and the foothills of Tycho convinced the four survivors that at least there was no more immediate danger. Eventually they felt justified in returning to normal routine.

It was several terrestrial days later that Professor Jantz took the opportunity afforded by Dr. Jackson's absence on a survey expedition to do some work of his own in the small underground laboratory. He was absorbed in the spectroscopic analysis of quantities of fine black dust.

When Captain Harper found him the professor was engaged in electronically heating a minute pile to incandescence.

"Which sample are you working on now?" asked Harper conversationally.

Professor Jantz displayed the pleasure of a child who has discovered something altogether wonderful in his Christmas stocking. "The third sample from cavern fourteen," he explained happily.

"How's it going?"

"My dear Harper, this is a perfect specimen of bituminous carboniferous coal of the type known as fusain. There is a wonderful abundance of microspores and macrospores. My theories, I may say, are confirmed up to the hilt. When I get back to Earth I shall read a paper to—"

"What does it mean, in plain language?" interrupted Harper.

"It means quite simply that the moon was once teeming with estuarine swamps. It means that billions of years ago the moon was a riot of evolving life forms. In short, we have accumulated enough evidence to shake modern astrophysical theory right to its foundations."

"Why isn't there any surface evidence of all this?"

"Because as the moon began to lose its atmosphere the intensifying sunlight generated spontaneous combustion. Half the so-called metoric dust is the ashes from what must once have been tremendous smoldering graveyards."

Harper grinned. "So now you'll be able to blast the armchair astronomers."

"I most certainly shall. I have enough data to make most of my illustrious colleagues feel that the time has come for them to enter mental institutions."

162

Captain Harper took a couple of folded typewritten sheets from his pocket. "I really hunted you out to show you the message I intend to transmit back to Organization Headquarters. If there's anything you wish to add you'd better say so. I shall have to send it in the next hour or so."

Professor Jantz took the sheets and read them quickly:

DISPATCH SEVEN

From: HARPER, CAPTAIN OF ADVANCE EXPEDITION, LUNAR BASE ONE. *To:* EXECUTIVE COUNCIL, EXPEDITION H.Q., EARTH

Since the destruction of the robot-manned outpost, Jackson and Pegram have made an extensive survey of the ground within a radius of one hundred miles of base. They have discovered no more alien tracks, other than those originating from the hemisphere, and no further signs of independent activity. We are confident, then, that it is safe for the second moonship to depart on schedule; and feel that the equatorial expedition may be undertaken in face of environmental hazards only.

We have examined the debris of the robot outpost, and have drawn the following conclusions:

1) The robots are not indigenous to the moon, since their construction would demand resources and a highly developed life form, of which there is no evidence.

2) Their construction is beyond the present developments of human science.

3) Since their outpost was exposed and unpressurized, the three so-called coffins appear to have been the "hibernation" chambers and electrical charging beds of the robots during the lunar night. Evidence of their electrical potential was obtained before the outpost was destroyed.

4) Assuming that the three previous hypotheses are substantially correct, we believe that at some time the moon received an extraterrestrial expedition, which left the robots for observational purposes and scientific investigation.

5) Since the robots took the initiative in attacking us it is probable that their creators conditioned the machines to react aggressively to any phenomena that might be interpreted as interference.

6) Bearing in mind that the robots were apparently equipped with space radio, it is probable that they originated within our own solar system.

The full arguments in support of these views will be submitted in Dispatch Eight. It remains for me to add our unanimous belief that the extra-terrestrial expedition will ultimately return to discover the fate of its mechanical outpost. It is hoped, by that time, that human beings and equipment will be present on the moon in sufficient force to fulfill our aims irrespective of interference or co-operation.

Professor Jantz looked up from the typewritten sheets. "I think you've given our main conclusions admirably," he said. "The rest can wait until we have time to prepare a full report. As soon as I've finished with these samples I'll put my own notes in order for you."

"It's about time Jackson and Pegram were back," remarked Harper, stuffing the sheets back in his pocket. "I'll give them a call on the transceiver."

He went out, leaving the professor to continue his work. For another two hours Jantz was able to go on with his analysis of the samples from cavern fourteen without being disturbed.

Then Captain Harper returned. "They got back safely," he announced.

"Good, good. Now we can relax for a few hours."

"They want us to go up to the surface," said Harper. "They say there's something worth seeing."

"More samples!" exclaimed the professor delightedly. "Where the devil did I put my headpiece?"

Presently the two men made their way through the airlock and clambered up the metal ladder set against the walls of the fissure. They reached the surface to see Jackson and Pegram standing by the lunar tractor.

"Have you found something interesting?" called Jantz hopefully over his personal radio.

"Yes," replied Jackson, raising his arm. "Look around."

Everywhere the shadows were stretched to unimaginable lengths and the rolling lava plains, softened now in oblique sunlight, were beginning to assume the dark contours of a lunar twilight. The scene was desolate, grotesque, and in its own fashion altogether beautiful.

Slowly, infinitely slowly, the sun began to sink over distant fire-tipped mountains. Slowly the great ball of Earth loomed against a star-strewn backcloth of total darkness.

Captain Harper and his three companions stood silently in a deepening green glow, watching the inexorable course of the sun over a ragged horizon.

It was a scene to be remembered as long as they lived—the subtle change stealing over a petrified landscape; the slow, impressive end of their first lunar day.

Watch for....

AFTER THE RAIN

by

John Bowen

A Ballantine "FIRST"
(#284K—35¢)

How would you react if you found yourself on a modern day Noah's Ark (with no foreseeable prospect of finding dry land?)

What would you think of to extend the limited supply of food?

Would you agree to separate sleeping quarters for male and female?

Would you *feel* that any human life you encountered was precious to the survival of the race, or would you want to kill all others in order to give yourself a better chance?

How would YOU survive?

BALLANTINE SCIENCE FICTION

Published through November, 1958